SAW

BY STEVE KATZ

First Edition
First Printing, 1998

Published by FC2
with support given by The English Department
Unit for Contemporary Literature of Illinois State University
and the Illinois Arts Council

Address all inquiries to:
FC2
Unit for Contemporary Literature
Campus Box 4241
Illinois State University
Normal, IL 61790-4241

Saw
Steve Katz

ISBN: 1-57366-046-9 (paperback)

Library of Congress Catalog Card Number
98-071786

Cover Design: Todd Michael Bushman

Produced and Printed in the United States of America

also by STEVE KATZ

The Exagggerations of Peter Prince

Creamy and Delicious

SAW

PREFACE

The order of these "reports" is arbitrary although their accuracy is strict. They can be read at any hour of the day and there is no time limit. The natural number and order of words in each report has been strictly regulated by universal laws that are presently being studied, and the events accounted for within each individual report are arranged in a sequence and system according to a code that isn't yet deciphered. Each report is numbered and those numbers may be disregarded since they were imposed on the text by myself as an expression of my personal fondness for a certain number.

I am not yet at liberty to divulge the manner in which these reports got to me, but I can freely reveal that some of them seem to be missing, though I don't know which ones. There may be more reports than presently meet the eye. Other languages are a distinct possibility. I have it from good sources that similar texts exist in the Russian, though their publication in a format like this, or in any other format, is highly unlikely.

One can speculate about the veracity of these contents and decide for himself, but whatever the conclusion it is still a matter of mystery that they exist at all, and in a form that can please or amuse us. Beyond the level of amusement, however, several serious questions arise. To whom does The Astronaut send these "reports"? How is the information contained in them deciphered? What could they mean? Does whoever receives them intend to act on them? Are we in danger? Is The Astronaut still around here somewhere? Why doesn't Eileen speak up?

I shrug my shoulders every time I think of these questions. If you see me shrug my shoulders you'll know what I'm thinking. This little apartment where I write on a card table is full of roaches. I've learned to smile at them. It doesn't hurt. This evening at 6:30 I'll have dinner with Steve Reich, the great composer. When I get back the roaches will be lively and will rush across the floor like fresh questions across my mind: Where does The Astronaut get some money? I shrug. Cars in the street slam into each other. I look out the window in time to see the stately Helgy Tendon step from a smashed Toronado. She shakes her head and looks up at my window. "I'm hurt, Steve, I've just had a bad accident." I let my long brown hair down out of the window so battered Helgy can climb the four stories to my apartment, and I treat her wounds. Her car is towed away and she is relieved not to have to park it this evening. I brew some tea and we watch for news on television.

17

LEROY

Eileen grabs a subway and heads for Van Cortlandt Park. What a park. Anything you want is there. Cricket. Lacrosse. Ladies' softball. "So enjoy yourself," mumbles Eileen, as she slides to a seat near the mucky window. The woman in the seat by the door reads the *New York Times*. Eileen hates that newspaper and all its contents. The pup she has hidden under her sweatshirt is wiggling. "Nice pup you got there, lady," says a black kid, edging toward her along the seats. He is wearing a baseball uniform, and The Marvels is the name of his team. "I've got no puppy here," Eileen replies, knowing pups are illegal on the subway.

The kid sends some gestures and winks back to his teammates at the other end of the car. "You've sure got something that whines and wiggles like a puppy under there."

Eileen ignores the kid. The IRT rumbles on down the track and busts into daylight, heading for the Bronx. The boy tries to pet the hidden pup with his first baseman's mitt. "I told you there is no puppy under there," Eileen insists, turning aside and looking hard out the window. Flat-topped buildings stick up all over the little hills of the Bronx. "If you don't got no puppy in there," says the kid, "with all that whining and whomping around in there, then you something boss, lady; you got the jivingest jugs in the world." The kid goes back to his teammates and they slap each other's palms and roll baseballs up their arms.

Eileen sets the puppy free in the park, and it yerps with joy. The sun is good and hot. She slips out of her sweatshirt and strolls up the paths toward granite cliffs and bushes. Her tight bell-bottom jeans make her feel free at the ankles, and her purple jersey polo shirt grazes the nipples of her small, braless bosom. She feels giddy and loose. The little pup jumps at her and scampers around and growls: a lively white and black beagle crossbreed pup with a warm tongue. High above them the sun lights the wings of a hawk that glides in wide circles on the air currents, not a twitch but for its head that flicks from side to side. Van Cortlandt Park, in New York City, is most famous for its hawks. They hunt there for pigeons and squirrels and other small stuff running on the rocky slopes. They swoop down on baseballs. They snatch the caps of nurses. A sandwich isn't safe. Eileen steps across the grass, skirts the baseball diamonds, keeps one eye peeled for the circling hawk. She heads for a point of seclusion and comfort up in the rocks. The sun is strong; the wind, fresh. Jet streams crosshatch the sky. Hawk lazes in his circles overhead, casual enough to make us foolhardy. Eileen pauses high on a rock to gaze south at Manhattan poking up through the smog. The city is a dumb bunch of things, she thinks, so filthy and crunchy in its thick sauce. Then she hears the puppy squeal as the big hawk yanks it off the ground in its talons. "Good boy," she says, and salutes the hawk who carries the pup to the top of some rocks.

Below her some stoned-out people swallow handfuls of pebbles for kicks. She certainly could never be one of them, nor one of any group she ever knew about. That was why she came to New York. She stretches her back out on a flat stone and a lovely depression floats down to settle around her like a heap of leaves. "Whatever my life is," she whispers into her mood, "nothing I do will ever add up to anything. No accounting. It's all for the moment, for the good moments. I'll never get to a conclusion. I won't reach a climax."

Hawk drops down softly to a fallen limb by her knee. "Thanks a million," it says. Eileen sits up. A bit of puppy gristle clings to the hook of the beak. "It sure is swell of you to keep on bringing me those tender pups. They make me feel so good. A hawk in New York is like a fish out of water these days. No eats here. Everything comes frozen or in cans."

Eileen smiles. "It's because I'm an Aquarius. My friend Corinne at the office is a Virgo, and she thinks what I do is hideous. But I don't balk at the law of tooth and fang. I tell my friends to feed the hawks and they think I'm a freak. I mean I believe violence is your predicament. It's in your nature. Once you make a hawk into a friend you can begin to understand him."

"I like you a whole lot, lady," says the hawk. "Otherwise I would let you know how stupid you are, because you are stupid. Violence is not even a word. We're up there for the circling, making the circles, that's where it's at."

"Maybe that's true, but I want to tell you something." Eileen is enthusiastic. "I really need to blow up the *New York Times*. Everyone would be much better off if it were a bunch of cinders. And then maybe some TV networks. Get rid of all of them. But it's the *Times* that's my biggest nemesis. Everybody reads it and stuffs his head full of information. What good is information to the people? All it does is prevent me from becoming an adventuress."

"Forget those half-assed ideas. I tell you, if human beings could learn to fly in circles of their own volition, life would be calm for them and information would fall away, and meaning would fall away, and wisdom would follow them like a stream of song. You humans are really out to lunch. There is no such thing as adventure."

"You yourself told me that the hunting was bad."

"Listen carefully. You're a nitwit. Hunting isn't worth the prey of a mantis in my estimation. It's not what you get. It's not the catch. It's the circling itself, those long arcs you can make without creaking a wing. I mean I like my food, lady, but that's not—"

"You should call me Eileen."

"Okay, Eileen. But there's nothing the matter with it if I don't eat. It's my least care. Usually one gets something to eat, and if he doesn't he just keeps circling and circling into the most exquisite dreams. Those are the circles I make, and those circles are my life, which is the moving circle of my horizon as I fly, which makes me harmonious with my world, the sphere. And the Earth arcs around the sun, and the universe warps out forever. I know all that. I didn't have to study mathematics. Eileen, my dearest human friend, you live in a box, and that's why you always get those headaches." With that final remark the hawk stretches his wings and a few powerful sweeps bear him aloft.

So she gets headaches, how does a hawk understand that? He gets into the air easily, and that's admirable, but what he has to say is just so much hawk breath. So she gets headaches. What does a hawk know about aspirin and the even more potent remedies? Pills are little circles in themselves. So what? Take all your hawk theories along with all your man theories and put them in orbit and what have you got? Solar garbage. What she still wants to do is burn down the *New York Times*. Hawks make easy assumptions about human life without ever pausing in their circles to examine the complexities. If she were shaped like a wheel things would be different.

Eileen strolls on the paths around the baseball diamonds. This is the first really "good" day of the year and she knows that something extraordinary is about to happen to her. If this were not LEROY but was instead a cheap movie that featured her, she could expect to make a stop at some storefront fortune teller on Second Avenue and have the old fraud read from a crystal ball, or from the tarot, or from the stars, or her palm, that she is obliged that day to meet a remarkable and confusing stranger. What a bore on a day so warm and sunny to be constrained to have conversations with someone remarkable, and a lot of superstitious nonsense anyway. Such hocus-pocus impresses the faint of heart, people who walk into lampposts and sit on wet park benches. All she wants to happen is something that keeps her from ever going back to her job again, that persistent nibbling just below the heart she has to call her "work." She loves to lie in the sun. She could be a professional lizard. Work is a stupid idea, a desiccating poison that people in this darkest of dark ages inflict on themselves.

"Hey lady, where's your pup?" The Marvels are on the playing field she passes, warming up for a game with the incomparable New York Bullets. "A hawk snatched it," she shouts back. "Right on, lady. We play The Hawks next Saturday." She feels something observing her. The boys toss around last year's baseballs, wrapped in black electrician's tape. They shag flies, do some pepper drill, practice sliding, bunting, learn to chew tobacco. Something is moving in the bushes, like a cloud. She heads for some flat rocks she knows about where she can lie down with her belly to the sun and no one will see her. There's a rumbling noise somewhere, like a jet plane, but it seems to be on the ground. She rises through some sumacs, some scruffy willows, some sycamores, and arrives at her flat place where the sun heats up her belly when she slips off her shirt and stretches out. She yawns, and almost dozes. Jets in great profusion rise above her belly from Kennedy, La Guardia and Newark, dropping poisonous smoke. She hears something else, like a large metal wheel cracking the gravel. "Who is it?" She pulls her shirt down. A big sphere rolls her way over the flat rocks. It's as high as she is, and full of a milky iridescence that looks like life. This is the most remarkable thing that has ever happened to her, and then the sphere begins to speak.

"I could have been quieter, but I was afraid that would alarm you completely. I've been gathering mushrooms."

"I'll bet you have," says Eileen.

"This time of year the morels pop up all over, and I know a spot that's just chock full of them. Nobody gets there before me. The month of May is so nice, just because of my favorite mushrooms."

The sphere makes Eileen smile. Almost immediately she forgets the fact that it's nothing but some big geometry with a voice. "You've got no way to pick mushrooms. You haven't any hands," she observes.

Waves of crimson, like a smoky blush, drift

through the sphere's interior, and he says, softly, "You would notice something like that right off. We all have limitations, but perhaps you noticed that I said 'gathered,' not 'picked.' It's a question of semantics."

Eileen sits there stymied for a moment beside the sphere. City noises rise in her ears. She doesn't understand what is going on. Here she is in an extraordinary situation and she reacts no more than as if she were bored by it. She's numb. A chill descends in her and she looks at the sphere and wishes it had some arms to throw around her immediately and comfort her. "I'm terrible company," she whispers. "I have so little to say."

"Don't let it bug you," says the sphere, rocking back and forth. "You get through to me without words. Conversation went out with the trolley car and the glass milk bottle, anyway." The sphere rolls a little closer to Eileen, as if to get more intimate. "Back then I used to talk all the time. I used to make predictions, like a clairvoyant, and I liked to tell them to people; for instance, my basic prediction was that in 1965 southern Japan and the Philippines were to sink in an horrendous earthquake that would give birth to seven new chains of populous islands. California was to rise twelve feet higher out of the sea, causing a man named F. Scott Fitzgerald (not the writer) to become fabulously wealthy from the treasures he finds heaved up on the extended shore by his modest beach house. How do you like that?"

"None of that ever came true, did it?"

"No. Of course not. But that was only part of it. Listen to this. The Galápagos were supposed to pop off the Earth like a cork and spin into orbit, shattering the moon and causing a dispersal of satellite fragments that would orbit the Earth like one of Saturn's rings. Half of the Pacific would flow into the hole left by the Galápagos. South America would stretch out. Atlantis rediscovered. The hollow Earth theory proved correct. Within the Earth such pressures would build up that geysers funnel out all over the globe: Poughkeepsie, Tel Aviv, Kuznetsk, La Paz, Oslo, Christchurch—everywhere—a thousand feet into the air, spewing out quantities of strange steamed artifacts, whose use couldn't be known on the surface but which clearly must be the product of some form of intelligent life inhabiting the center of the globe."

"That's it." Eileen points a finger at the sphere. "You're from the center of the earth."

"You're right as rain. Very smart," says the sphere. "I left to escape the cataclysm, and also to see if the rumors of intelligent life on the outer surface were true."

"Were they?"

"Partially true, as far as I can tell. A lot of coquetry, willfulness, anger, and confusion. How about this prediction: By 1970 every city was going to have moving sidewalks, so nobody would have to walk to the store unless he wanted to get there twice as fast, and other people would get about on what looked like jet-propelled pogo sticks, making densely populated areas look like popcorn machines."

"That didn't come true either."

"Nope. But I predict that Mao Tse-tung and Chiang Kai-shek will be dead by 1985."

Eileen smiles. "There's a chance for that one, anyway. But I'm really more interested in you. Do you have parents in there? What are they like?"

"Of course I do. They're just some parents. Authoritarian. Rigid. Dense. My father was a pyramid and my mother was rhomboid. The last thing they expected to have was a sphere, and they had no idea how to cope with me. As soon as I could roll off on my own I put distance between us."

"Don't you ever have a hankering to return to the center of the Earth, to be with your own kind?"

"Rarely. I don't think that way. I am my own kind. I prefer isolation. It amuses me to be out here, and there are mushrooms, like little friends. The little fellows grow on the inner surface as well, you know. I guess they grow in pairs." The sphere starts slowly rolling up the hill, and Eileen follows. "But let me finish giving you my major prediction. You see, that catastrophe was supposed to wipe out most of the population of the U.S., leaving only teamsters and athletes to pick up the pieces, with some high-ranking military. They start again through a tribal system. They remember only sixteen letters of their alphabet, rendering the three books they find hermetically sealed in a capsule less than useless. *The Best of Broadway: 1954, Aion* by C. G. Jung, and *Born to Raise Hell*, a study of Richard Speck, the mass murderer, are the books. None of this came true, however. Does it bother you to hang out with a sphere whose predictions don't come true?"

"Of course it doesn't." Such a gentle presence is the sphere she walks beside. Variations of color that she imagines her eyes invent appear in its interior as it speaks. She strokes its surface affectionately and it quivers like a membrane. "No sphere has ever spoken with me before."

"Isn't that odd," says the sphere. "And you, what were your parents?"

"Just poor Midwestern people. My mother was pretty and my father handsome. I inherited their looks, for whatever it's worth. I lead a stupid life. I'm nobody."

"If you are nobody, what am I? Just geometry in your world. No body."

"I'm sorry," says Eileen, blushing deeply. "That was a dippy thing to say."

They come to the top of the hill and the sphere stops. "Amazing," it says. "Remarkable."

"What is?" Eileen looks around.

"Your city. Look at the way that Manhattan

has disappeared down there. It has disappeared. That's miraculous." The sphere spins with excitement. "You know, one of my predictions was that Manhattan would disappear in the late sixties or early seventies. I predicted that it would dissolve in its own air and wash away, and now look. It's true. It's gone. My prediction has come true and I'm so happy. You are my good luck charm."

The sphere is right. Manhattan does seem to have disappeared, though she knows it isn't gone for good. Just a storm has swaddled it in clouds, rushing in off the Atlantic and sending a thick tongue up the Harlem River towards the Bronx. "That's just the rain on the city. You can hear thunder."

"Oh thunder. Right. Rain. There's always some damned explanation. I'm still not used to it here. Well, the rain can have Manhattan, damn it. I'm wrong again."

"I would have been quite upset," says Eileen, "had Manhattan actually disappeared. I would have been left without anything. Not even a friend."

"Well, then I'm glad my prediction didn't come true. To hell with it. I won't make any more. But I still think something is going to happen, and I'd like to know what it is."

"I predict we'll get soaked if we stay here," says Eileen, getting back into her sweatshirt.

"I don't get wet," says the sphere. "I can be impermeable."

"Maybe I sound fussy, but I'll get soaked and chilled, and I just got over a cold. I'm going to get to the subway before it rains."

"I even like the fresh water on my surface," the sphere says.

Eileen feels reluctant to leave the sphere. She knows the encounter will seem another of her daydreams once several hours have passed. She wants to touch it some more and to hear it talk. "Please . . . umh . . ." she finds the words difficult to release. "Please come home with me to my apartment if you want."

The sphere bounces around in place as if it has been bobbled. "I was hoping you would ask me to come. I haven't seen many interiors."

Eileen strokes the sphere with both her hands. "Well," she says. "One doesn't often find a sphere in the park she feels she can invite to her home."

Eileen loves the people of her adopted city. If she turned up with a sphere in her hometown of Swisher, Iowa, the whole population would call her a Communist Hippie Beatnik and they never would have a minute's privacy, but here she gets only a few glances over the shoulders from New Yorkers who shrug. Eileen is actually the only one who pays attention to her unusual escort. She gets a sense of vertigo from its rolling motion, because she imagines it continually turning its head over and getting dizzy. That clearly isn't the case. The mental parts, where the senses are, from which it communicates, is probably at the very center where she guesses it is soft, but the surface is tough, though she notices it can vary its texture for her touch, changing from soft to slick to plush to rigid. What a companion it is for her hands. She still feels dizzy with it, like a little girl doing cartwheel after cartwheel on the lawn. The sphere pops up and settles on the seat opposite her and remains there despite the jolting of the IRT.

"How do you stay up there?" she asks.

"Stay up where?"

"On the seat, when the subway jerks? You look like you should just roll off."

"I never think about it," says the sphere. "I have no reason to roll off, so I don't roll off, but I can understand why you wonder about it. When I first started living on the surface I used to wonder how you kept balanced on those two posts. I kept expecting you to fall off, but you never did."

Eileen's life seems as if she is finally having the experiences she bargained for. Spicy. If the sphere, once they get home, makes a pass at her, well, that is what she has come to New York for, to get away from the humdrum routines of monotonous Midwestern life. They get off at 79th Street and Broadway and walk the few blocks north to her apartment, under a sky that is clearing as fast as it has clouded up, the smell of ozone, the washed air, the sunlight flying down on glowing buildings. Her little apartment house is wet and luminous.

"You taking such a thing with you to your apartment?" asks the lady with a little yellow dog, that Eileen frequently greets on the street. "To your apartment? You must have a big apartment."

"It's coming home with me like a friend."

"What should it be?" The old woman slips on her glasses. "What kind of a thing do you call that?"

"This is my friend, the sphere, Mrs. . . ."

"Lubell. Mrs. Lubell, mother of Harry Lubell the TV producer. So what is this, anyway? Is this what you kids start to see from squirting the mayonnaise into your veins?"

"I'm hardly a kid, Mrs. Lubell."

"I didn't mean you, darling. But those kids, they get these hypodermics and then they jab themselves with cranberry juice and chloroform. Who knows what else? There's one of them in my house and what he sees is a special thing."

"Well, you see this sphere, don't you?"

"I don't see nothing. Don't ask me what I see. You're better off if you don't see nothing these days."

Though it's too wide for the doorways the sphere fits through each one as if it doesn't exist. It pauses by the sill of her apartment as she switches on some lights. "I've never spent any time in one of these interiors before," the sphere says. Eileen is suddenly embarrassed. The place isn't herself. She has never done the decoration she always promised. The dead walls are covered with a dog-eared poster of Lenny Bruce, a dull batik hanging, a picture of the Rolling Stones. Nothing herself. The sphere moves around, humming and glowing like a detective's device, then it pauses before a little fishbowl full of brightly colored transparent marbles. "This is just amazing," it says. "If you had these where I come from you'd be locked up." The sphere stops moving and talking. Silence rushes in on them, separating them with the random noise of the building at dinner time. Eileen chews up some bread and cheese she has brought from the kitchen. The sphere seems to be watching her. It rolls onto the coffee table and amuses itself by balancing on the edge. It must be taking some account of how she has fitted out her life, and she doesn't know how to explain that this place isn't what she really is, but just a way station, a watering hole she was stopping at on her journey to wherever. She begins in the silence to feel the panic of losing contact. Nothing is right. Her own apartment is unreal, like the lair of a hibernating beast. She shuts her eyes for a moment and feels herself rolling over and over, as if the sphere has got into her. "Don't you ever feel peculiar?" she says, when she opens her eyes. "I mean you're here on the surface of the Earth, where you don't belong, without friends, or hope of anyone to understand you."

"That makes little sense to me." The voice of

the sphere projects a calm that slows her uneasiness. "Everything I do is interesting to me. I have everything I need. I have myself. I don't stay still."

"I am . . . I have nothing," Eileen says slowly, wholeheartedly, as if she is blowing a great weight off her tongue. "You're so lucky not to be made of this flesh. All I feel in myself is an endless dissolution, like I'm run through with nematodes and being carried away from myself in little nibbles, off into a void. I know despair is fatuous, but every face you look at is destroyed by troubles, and behind those troubles lies an abyss. You're lucky just to be a visitor. Nothing is strong enough to hold me together. I don't even know what I'm talking about, and why I say it to a sphere. What are you, or what am I for that matter? If there were another world I'd like to go there and try it for myself, because I don't sit very easy in this one. I want to know some whole people, but there just don't seem to be any. Just nerve bunches, like transmitters running with shapes inflicting pain. Everyone is suffering, and it's like that suffering is a skyscraper built around us in our sleep and only a certain dream we can never have in this life will remove it. I'm so unsettled. I need to blow up the *New York Times*. I need to go away. My friends talk revolution. The only revolution can be a breakthrough to what's real. I care about that. Something durable has to come clear. What's to become of us? I feel something supreme and horrible is happening on the Earth, and we will be excluded. Flesh. How did you ever get into my house, you roly-poly? This must sound so stupid to you. It's like car horns. People talk like honking taxis. Honk. Out of my way. Blast. This is ridiculous to a sphere. I don't know what I talk about. I just want to find any other world, someplace calmer. I want space to unload, anywhere. You find me tiresome."

The sphere rolls toward her till it is touching her and it moves around her softly grazing her clothes. "You get so serious," it says. "Just relax. You should laugh a lot. Flesh is flesh. It's like the air. Some day you'll get along without it but for now there is no way to step outside, because it's inside of you. You have it and it has you, like a lover, or a talent. Relax. There's nothing to resist." The sphere keeps rubbing her while he makes gentle philosophy. She begins to feel sexy. Perhaps the sphere is just handing her a line, she thinks, and wants only to get her into bed. She feels a pleasant tingling all over her skin. It can't be just a sphere of philosophy that makes her feel this way. The doubts and troubles she has fetched from deep within are slowly displaced by a round, rising dreamlike motion in herself. "You . . . you touch me like . . . like this," she says.

"You need to be touched. I know that," says the sphere. "Those feelings reach me quicker than words. Perhaps through the language understanding may grow, but knowledge descends through touch alone."

"I know what you are," Eileen says lightly. "You're a spherical make-out artist, playing out a line for me."

"A line?"

"It makes no difference. Forget about it. Did you ever make love to a human woman before?"

"In the park once I made love, if that's what you call it, but that was long ago and I think it was a young human male."

"You think it was a 'young human male.' What are you, a female?"

"Of course not. I'm a sphere, as you see me."

"A queer sphere," Eileen claps her hand over her mouth. "You would do it with men or women."

"Of course I'd 'do it' with men or women, or with dogs."

"With dogs?"

"They seem to be everybody's favorite. In the park you see men with men, women with women. You see everybody with dogs."

"Golly," Eileen blushes. "Sometimes I forget I'm just a hayseed girl from Swisher, Iowa, but it's true. My friend, Lester Stueval, used to talk about doing it with young sows. He was far out." Eileen begins to circle the sphere. The sexiness she feels is uncontrollable, but nothing sticks out on the sphere, nothing to grab or stroke. Its surface slowly changes texture in the most pleasing way, and as she strokes it she feels mild electricity flowing just under her skin. She starts it rolling toward her bedroom, her excitement whetted by questions that stroke her mind: How can this sphere ever penetrate her? Would she call it sex with a sphere? If her experience were ever jotted down by a writer, could it be called pornography by the millions?

Once in the bedroom she quickly undresses, a strange activity before a sphere, who seems to get naked from within, its most intimate substances seeping to the surface. The skin is so inadequate, she thinks, in order to be genuinely naked she would have to remove it. The sphere rolls toward her and she spreads her arms as it touches her. "Do something," she says.

"I want to," says the sphere. "You're so sweet and gorgeous."

Her body feels shot through with refreshing, vital warmth, and she swoons backward onto the floor, but something soft breaks her fall. The sphere rolls up and down her body in a perfect, gentle massage, slowly intensifying its action and making her feel covered head to toe with a warm, satiny fabric, and all her bones feel as if they have been turned loose in her muscles and rolled down a hill. Suddenly the sphere seems to be not only on top of her but under her also, rolling in two directions at once. She feels a minute massaging just under her skin, and begins to let out little shudders of sighs and screams, and she suddenly feels safe inside the sphere rolling over and over down a long hill picking up speed like a juggernaut in ecstasy. She opens her eyes on the marvelous incandescence of the room generated by the sphere who is setting itself off in pale vermilion bubbles toward the ceiling. In a moment her eyes close again and she falls asleep and continues to talk with the sphere in a dream. "Have you ever been in love?" she asks. "What is love?" it responds. "Have you ever been hungry?" "What is hungry?" "Have you ever been tired?" "What is tired?" "Have you ever been angry?" "What is angry?" "Have you ever thought of marriage?" "What is marriage?" "Have you ever had the religious experience?" "What is experience?" In the dream Eileen and the sphere circulate in empty space, and they never touch, though they resemble each other, and Eileen feels closer to the sphere than she has ever felt to father or lover.

By morning the sphere has fled but Eileen isn't disappointed. She feels permanently changed, lifted like a wing off the planet onto another realm. She is curious to go outside and see what it is all about again. A fringed buckskin miniskirt, a yellow silk tasseled blouse, thin-strapped high-heeled Italian sandals, a lime-green silk scarf around her neck, in the mirror she looks too appealing to hit the street. She feels divine. Out she goes. A rare crisp morning after a night of rain has clarified the air. The people take long strides or short quick steps with dogs bounding at their sides. No one looks lazy. Up and down Broadway troops of colorful people walk their dogs and whistle. Eileen heads north, thinking of something to buy. She has left her purse at home with no money in it. Old people walk their Pomeranians and Schnauzers. Pretty girls heel their German Shepherds. Hookers walk their Doberman Pinschers. Drag Queens strut with Great Danes. Elegant ladies with Afghan and Borzoi. Chummy animals, all of them, and full of teeth which they bare at Eileen because they hate her. Eileen has already taken her step off the Earth and she drifts up Broadway, sexy and vulnerable. They look her over, the stoned young couples, the old women in loose cotton dresses, the young men from behind their shades. They're like snipers. They're wallflowers taking tithes from her skin. How glad she is to have left behind this life of sinister presences, this uptown Broadway hanging out, this looking through sunglasses, this weather. She is being followed. Seven blocks and the same male behind her. What could she want now with a male? A confusing pursuit. She walks more quickly and he continues to get closer. He is just behind her. She can hear his clothes. She turns around.

"I am The Astronaut," he says. He is a small, handsome man.

"What's your reason for following me? I have nothing for you."

"Now that I am here you no longer can be the main character of LEROY."

Eileen is startled by such a twist, though not upset. She has no ambitions to be the main character of anything. Now that the sphere has changed her life she would prefer more time to herself. Her sphere is gone forever, she realizes, and she feels ready to weep. "What do you mean by that?" she asks.

"Don't let it trouble you. I am here now and must replace you as the protagonist of LEROY."

Since she has come to New York City, Eileen muses, each thing that happens to her has been stranger than the last. "If this is true, what do I do now?"

"You do what you please. You may leave, or remain in LEROY as a secondary personage. I should like to see you from time to time."

"How do you know this is what happens?" Eileen asks.

"I have the ability to read ahead."

"Why do you claim that you are The Astronaut?"

"That's who I am. There hasn't been space yet to explain how it happens that I am, but I am always The Astronaut."

"I guess it's quite simple and clear-cut, except that before you take over I'd like to ask you to help me with one thing."

"Certainly," says The Astronaut. "As long as we can take care of it on this page."

"I still need to blow up the *New York Times*."

"That will be no problem," says The Astronaut. Eileen is jubilant. She shoves her arm through his and they head for the downtown IRT. Forty-three minutes later the *New York Times* is a heap of rubble.

EXPLANATION A

Some explanation for the presence of The Astronaut is in order. How did he get here? Why is he here? What will he be up to during his stay? Is he merely a voyeur or shall we add him to the other threats to our existence: radiation, DDT, thermal pollution, boring politicians, famine . . . endless paralyzing enumeration. Before you ask about The Astronaut you ought to question yourself. Are you paranoid? Are you a liberal? Are you disgustedly rich? How do you spend your first hour in the morning? Are you shamefully poor? Do you stand on your head? Do you gather force through meditation? Do you call your horse down from the pasture? Is your bath long and luxurious? Are you a revolutionary? Do you notice the light? Who are your friends? Do any of them make you uncomfortable? What will you sacrifice for them? Have you ever confessed your maliciousness? Do your friends recognize your beatitude? Would you rather be a bird? Are you an angry if distant witness to injustice? Do you take too much dope? Too little dope? Are you a child or a grownup? How far will you be pushed before you take a stand? Do you pamper yourself? Did you ever consider becoming an artist? Do you know that art will set you free? Does it feel good to complain? Are you threatened? Are you disappointed? How many comforts can you give up before life is no longer worth living? Are you witty? Do you laugh? Have you got five dollars? Will you give it to me? Have you ever stolen for the fun of it? Do you steal to live? Have you ever been beaten? Are you beaten now? What's your name? Are you hungry? Will you have a place in the new society? Under what conditions would you kill a man, a rabbit, a fox terrier? Have you lost interest in The Astronaut? Where do you live at this moment?

The Astronaut visits our Earth from a distant galaxy where the inhabitants are as different from us as we are from an undersea mountain's comprehension of snow. They live in their galaxy as we live on our planet, moving among various clusters of stars as we move from continents to islands. Their scale is so immense that were a human in the presence of one of them he could never detect it, their matter being too diffuse for our senses; each immense molecule would come on as a star, and someone would cry out that new constellations were suddenly sprouting in our own sky, and just as suddenly they would disappear, leaving a track of madness on the earth. They are evolved creatures who live together harmoniously in a state of benign anarchy, free from conflict, without malice, self-governing. They admire one another forever. Their problems arose only when they began to have trouble reproducing. They don't reproduce as humans do through the physical act of sexual intercourse, though it does take at least two of them to accomplish reproduction. A new creature of their kind is more a product of mind, a perfect conception achieved initially, perhaps, by one of them and communicated to another (there is no differentiation by sex among them, only by a kind of wave-pattern emission through which they ascertain compatibility for reproduction). When the notion of the new being is totally conceived by one, and then communicated in all its details to another, happily absorbed and admired, till it becomes a clear conception in the mate's mind, then the new individual sets out on the slow process of birth. The extraordinary qualities of The Astronaut, for example, can be accounted for by the fact that he was the result of simultaneous ideation in the minds of two individuals at once (his "mother" and "father"), who will remain nameless, because the names of these beings can often cause synapses to fuse in the human mind. The Astronaut was so clear and perfect an idea that through a process we might call meditation his "parents" launched him immediately on the road of concrescence. Among those creatures there is no growth in size, but rather a process of substantiation within a form that is full grown from its conception, like a jar that can fill itself with honey. It's not quite that simple, either, because the creature is "filled out" from the beginning, but the nature of his substance goes through several metamorphoses. It must be understood that nothing is quite so simple as this bare sketch makes it seem, because that other life smothers the richest analogy with its complexity.

Everyone must still wonder what The Astronaut is doing on Earth, so far from his Mother Galaxy, where he can be happy. Again the answer is both simple and complicated. The population of Mother Galaxy is decreasing. A crisis exists in the most crucial stage of their growth, the penultimate one, just before they become "flesh." At that stage they are composed of a substance that resembles snow, though it isn't cold nor is it even made of matter. It lies loosely heaped like unsorted thoughts within the already established form. The process of becoming a grownup consists in slowly sorting this substance till an order comes clear, a rigorous consistency they call adulthood. This process is becoming less frequent on Mother Galaxy. The creatures are reaching the snowlike consistency, and then slowly melting away, never to be heard of again, because individuals can never be repeated there. After much research they found that an infinitesimal quantity of a certain substance was lacking in the constitution of their snow stage that is absolutely necessary to catalyze the final process of substantiation. We can call it a substance by analogy, but it isn't actually that. It's more like a mode of thought, for the beings of Mother Galaxy don't actually consist of "substance" as we conceive it, but of modes, or potentialities that they can will to be more or less concrete. You can see how frail analogies are. The supply of this "substance" in their galaxy is almost totally exhausted, and The Astronaut is the one who in his perfection actually chose himself to leave Mother Galaxy in order to scour the universe in search of what they need.

Other problems, like how he got to Earth, and how he can be seen if in reality he is so huge, also demand our attention. Space travel, first of all, is no problem for these creatures. It's as easy for them to learn as it is for us to learn to tack against the wind. Once the notion suggests itself to them they can be gone. The reason they aren't seen more frequently at the various watering spots in the cosmos is because they are so happy and consider Mother Galaxy so bountiful, spacious, and various that they see no reason to go elsewhere. The Astronaut would never have traveled if it weren't for their dire shortage. In that case Eileen would still be in LEROY in major proportions.

The paradox of The Astronaut's size is also as simple as it is complex. Though he is huge as any of his fellow beings Eileen perceives him more or less as a pipsqueak. We can begin by heeding the old adage: "When in Rome do as the Romans do." On Earth that advice is a matter of willpower, manners, and diplomacy. For a cosmic traveler it's a law without exception. Being doesn't manifest itself in the same mode in every pocket of the universe, though it is manifest everywhere, no place can be outside it, nothing differentiated from it; but modes of manifestation seem to be predetermined (karmically determined) at given locations. The only way The Astronaut can be known on such a place as Earth is through a mode of being manifest on Earth. So many voyagers must pass through, causing nothing more than a twinkle in our minds, if even that. The Astronaut decided to stop here, to know the place and be known, and the best way that becomes possible on Earth is through the mode of flesh: human flesh. So here he is, a small fleshy person. Eileen has met him, has been usurped by him, and even though our contact shall be indirect, we shall know him. His immensity surrounds us, perhaps, but as we perceive him he is just a man, and as we come to know him he will be the star of LEROY. What better place for The Astronaut to solve the problems of Mother Galaxy than here on Mother Earth, and what more comfortable berth than right here in LEROY?

If you are thinking that LEROY is more science fiction, please drive that notion back from your mind. LEROY is the truth, recorded simply as I have come to know it. I shall never go near the science fiction genre. I don't dislike science fiction, but I find such stretching of the truth repugnant to my common sense and counter to my lifelong drive, which is to know and understand the world as it is. LEROY consists of what I understand in the world, what I have clearly seen, if not understood, but can clearly describe, and what I know others have seen, taken only from trustworthy sources.

By the way, the "substance" The Astronaut is looking for is an amalgam of ambition, greed, bullshit, pride, envy, bourbon, and smut, all of which he finds on Earth in immense quantities, though he hasn't yet figured how to separate it from the people so it will be available in a form he can cart home.

5

A FLY IN THE LEROY

"What I have here, what I've got for myself is a whale of a fly, and I'm not kidding myself," murmurs Stanley Federglans. He circles his desk and gleams at a plump, hairy fly squatting on his open letters. "He's probably skimming those letters," Stanley tells himself as he watches the fly wipe the haze from its eyes.

"Mr. Benjamin from Plastic Futures," the new secretary sings over the intercom.

"Tell Mr. Benjamin to go sniff glue, Miss Roquefort. Goddamit. This is a double fly. You come in yourself and get a load of my little buzzer."

"I haven't been here long, Mr. Federglans, but I know it would be counterproductive to insult this account."

"If you weren't the best in the business," Mr. Benjamin springs in through the door as the fly buzzes to the next letter. Stanley scoops it onto a three-by-five card and flips it into a half cup of cold coffee where it splashes around in desperation. "I'd take this job elsewhere. You'd better have something good to show me."

"Don't frustrate yourself. We're working like little elves. Here," he says to the secretary. "There's a fly in my coffee. Scoop it out for me, will you?"

"I'll just flush the beast down the toilet with the coffee." She turns on her heel.

"I want my fly back, Lillian. You know that."

"That's the way to treat a favorite; drown him in the coffee," says Mr. Benjamin. He walks around the room, scrutinizing the huge portraits of insects on the walls. "Treat your clients the same way and then see." Mr. Benjamin lifts some papers off a drawing board. "Are these designs for me?"

"Do you think that's for *me?* That's all yours. Look it over. It's the best work in the world. It's elegant, the information is right out in front. It's convincing, and it's got that special zonk."

"Here's your fly," says the secretary, flicking it onto his blotter from a plastic spoon.

"You're sure it's the same fly?" asks Stanley.

"It's got the same expression on its face," she says.

"Hey, beautiful," says Mr. Benjamin. "You're just the girl for whom I've been looking. Come with me to the new factory in North Carolina. Those little miniskirts—wow. What do you say?"

"Only if I can bring my own fly," the secretary says over her shoulder, as she bounces out of the office.

"She's a piece of ass, too," says Mr. Benjamin.

"I try not to notice the girls in the office," says Stanley.

Both men watch the wet spot spread slowly around the fly as it carefully wipes the coffee muck out of its hairs. "This fly is meticulous. I'd like to quit my job and devote myself. I'd write poems."

"Okay, now, business before poetry. These sketches here look like some modern art to me," says Mr. Benjamin. "I mean I'm in love with modern art, but when it comes to business I need to understand something. This industrial park is my pride and joy."

"Like me and my fly," says Stanley. He breathes on his creature to speed its drying. "Work is such a bore, anyway."

"Come off it and just explain something. I'm no artist, commercial or otherwise, but I'm paying for this. Put it in plain language."

"Fear not, mogul. You'll blow every mind in plastics with this approach. I invented that lettering." He bends over his darling again. "A sturdy little bug."

"I'm not convinced."

The noise of an antiwar demonstration in Times Square seeps through the seams of the curtain walls and sealed windows. The Astronaut strolls at the curb examining the demonstrators.

"If a fly could speak, he would explain this work of genius."

"This fly would tell you to buzz off." Mr. Benjamin laughs.

"Please. This is no average philistine fly you meet of a summer's day near a cow-flop in a pasture."

"Those were the days," a voice pipes up.

"This fly I discovered on my kitchen window. It was in a trance."

"If you had left me there a little longer I would have broken that window," says the fly, stepping off the wet spot.

"The fly speaks," Mr. Benjamin gasps. "Suddenly we've got a type of fly that speaks and I'm delighted to be here. We can tour the world."

"Not me. I prefer my own species. I'd like a nice piece of buzz."

"A horny individualist fly. I like him a lot," says Mr. Benjamin. "I've always had a question for a fly. Tell me, when we see two of you zizzing on top of one another, is that what it is?" He winks.

"This is bad company," mumbles the fly.

"I'm so insensitive," says Stanley. "All this time you wanted a mate."

"Hey. Maybe this fly can give us a hand," says Mr. Benjamin. "What do you think of this artwork, promotion-wise?"

The fly sniffs at a crumb on the desk. "I don't know enough about it."

"I'll fill you in." He turns to Stanley. "You listen too." He squats down so he's eyeball to eyeball with the fly. "This project is my special baby. I don't know if you understand how a man gets into business and has certain ambitions. He's a good man, but he puts on blinders to race after his goal. He becomes even a little ruthless, hurts some people, even his old chums. He is pursuing his dreams, so he forgets the human element. That's a description of my life up till now."

"Get to the point. A fly's life is short."

"Right. I understand that. So is mine. That's why I want the human element to be my first priority. Profit sharing, reasonable housing, culture. The whole *shtick.* We want to fill the world's dreams with benevolent plastics. That's why I'm speechless when I talk about it, and this promotion has to be like a plastic bible, a book of prophecy. It has to be catchy." Mr. Benjamin grins and sits back.

"Well, what are you thinking?" Stanley asks the fly.

The fly leaps to the mouth of an open ketchup bottle on Stanley's desk. "Abandon the project."

Mr. Benjamin's eyes fly open, and he slaps his hands to his cheeks. "Oy. 'Abandon,' he says. Abandon the promotion?"

"Abandon the whole plastics industry," says the fly, jumping up and down on the bottle.

"What's your name, fly?" says Mr. Benjamin. "That's no way for a fly to talk. What's your damned name?"

The fly ignores him and steps into the heart of the bottle.

"O my God. I'm so sick of it. How would you like a big thumb in your eye, goddamit? Do you think they even let a fly talk in China? Who do you think pays the bills?" Mr. Benjamin purses his lips and shouts as loud as he can into the bottle.

The fly rushes out onto Mr. Benjamin's lower lip. "It was a dark day for my people, Benjamin, when you all started putting garbage into plastic bags. Then they burn that plastic and throw poison plastic smoke into the air where we hang out."

Mr. Benjamin spits the fly off his lip and it lands on his eyeball. He grabs for it but it streaks back into the bottle.

"That fly is right," says Stanley Federglans, standing up tall. "And he's got the guts to speak out. I'm on his side. I'm abandoning."

"You swine. You're taking the side of a fly."

Stanley turns to the window. Noise from the demonstration below creeps through the seams of the building and in through his nose to his heart which is pumping comfortably in his chest. He smiles inwardly.

"Our contracts, Federglans, are airtight. You can't abandon the project. I'll tie you up in knots like a noodle," Mr. Benjamin threatens.

"Off the contracts. That's my favorite fly. He's like my inner voice that got stuck in my throat."

Mr. Benjamin picks up the intercom and speaks into it calmly. "Lillian, please call my office and have them contact each member of the board. I also want to talk with your boss's boss." He turns off the intercom and looks at Stanley Federglans. "Damn the artistic mentality," he snorts.

"If that fly departs the bottle with a different notion then I'll do what he says. Otherwise I'm not even here."

. . .

Names of the war dead scale the pearly face of the Allied Chemical building. The Astronaut watches them go up. Each has six jointless legs, no eyes, scarlet bodies shaped like droplets. They disappear into the sky. The Quakers and war resisters take turns announcing those names in a monotone over a feeble PA system. Seventh Avenue and Broadway pass through each other, surrounding the narrow island on which everybody stands. A few tourists, starchy, blond, discreet in their leisure-time fashions, cross Broadway to stare at the demonstrators. Their brother fights in this war. He's a pilot, they tell the dark aggressive girl who approaches them. She shudders when she hears it. They say they want him to come home. They excuse themselves when she starts to harangue them with her measured hysteria, because it is 1970, and they have given themselves only three days to do all of New York City. Six huge compressors kick off after lunch and Times Square sounds like the engine room of an oil tanker. "Faggots," shouts one tattooed man doing handstands around the demonstrators. "Mickey Mouse." The Tactical Police Force leans against some vans, smoking, rushing in and out of Nathan's with hot dogs in their gloved hands. The Astronaut pauses by a movie theater and notices that *The Vixen* is being shown. He enters and finds the screen amusing, especially the abundant flesh-colored light. When he gets back to the street the police are dragging away some of the demonstrators. People are wounded. A man with a hissing "s" reads off the names of the Smiths who were killed in the war. The Astronaut heads up 43rd Street and steps into the crowded doorway of a building. The elevator is full of elbows.

Fly keeps to the bottle. New people pack the office like winds crowding a cave. The Astronaut inserts himselr. Blank pages, paper cups, old designs whip through the air, pelting the newcomers. A severed arm spins across the room, spraying blood. "That's from my right shoulder," screams a young militant. He pounds the desk top with his remaining fist. "Where did all these people come from?" shouts Mr. Benjamin. A President's daughter crosses the room. She's bare from the waist up. "Nice tits," mutters Mr. Benjamin. She waves, on the end of a letter opener, the tongue she has torn from the mouth of her favorite folksinger. "This was supposed to be a quiet conference," Mr. Benjamin pleads. The singer has stuffed his mouth with a bandana and he wags his head in rhythm picking his guitar for the old lady from the DAR. She sits in a corner on a three-legged stool and weeps, and intones: "More fresh fruit. More white paper. More snappy salutes." Between everyone's legs crawls the mediator, honking like a taxicab. "Who the fuck is down there?" demands an ambitious woman. He bites into her naked calf and strips off a length of muscle as she continues to wipe her violet lenses.

These are stockholders, all of them—mistresses of landlords, fancy divorcées, the pick of the crop, children of the upper crust. Ambassadors show up out of nowhere. The Senators' amanuenses enter like potentates. "Even if this fly does talk," says a former candidate for mayor, "I shall still want to be convinced. A lot of talk goes on these days, but very little is done about it." The President's daughter dips the tongue she wields into an inkwell and "x's" out the insect portraits around the room. She hands the brush to John Q. Public—"Paint my knockers," she insists.

The fly hangs upside down in the bottle and snoozes. It drops off, kicks itself upright, lets out a soft bzzzzz, and then snubs the commotion in the room. "Wait," says Stanley Federglans, and he rushes to peer into the bottle.

"When can we split for the country, Auntie?" asks the child actress. "I want my cocaine."

"The man from the Pentagon is here, a Colonel Krispie," says the secretary, "and I'm going home. It's past five."

"Oy vay, that's impossible," says Mr. Benjamin. "I'm in absolute need of a shave, and I was going to get a haircut. Four days without a haircut. Today I look like a hippie."

A young woman bends over a pentagram she has drawn on the rug, and she rattles a tambourine and chants, her long black hair hiding her face.

"I will become the sun," a young man shrieks as he soaks his new tie-dye in lighter fluid, ignites it, and lifts it above his head on a T-square.

"Boring to fuck is what you are, brother," says the youth's little sister, lying on the floor, her pelvis still jumping. "I want more action."

A muscular female literary critic slips out of her bell-bottoms and whips a dildo from her dispatch case. "I won't pass this one up."

"Is this supposed to be an orgy?" asks a nearby agronomist.

"How can you be sure the fly is indeed in the bottle?" queries the Prof., resting in New York for his sabbatical year. "And once he gets out can we call him the same fly?"

"Dammitall," says Colonel Krispie, moving to the forefront. "This has got to cease and desist." He rips through the blue gauze the young witch has thrown over his eyes and makes a threatening gesture at the bottle.

"Stop that warmonger," shouts Stanley Federglans. "He'll bruise my fly."

"We have ways to make it talk," says the colonel. "Our national defense priorities cannot be undermined by a speechless fly in a bottle." Colonel Krispie grabs the bottle by the throat, turns it upside down, and shakes it till the ketchup flops onto the desk. With a great effort the fly swims loose of the ketchup and rushes back into the bottle. It lets out a few barely audible buzzes, bringing an inundation of silence down on the room. "Bzzzzz."

"Maybe now," says Stanley Federglans.

"This is nothing." The Astronaut inserts himself between the crowd and the fly. "Absolutely human zero."

"Who is this?" Stanley Federglans demands.

"The Astronaut," says The Astronaut.

"What's an Astronaut doing in my office? Get away from my fly. Go back to the moon."

The Astronaut grabs a brass bookend from the desk and smashes the bottle with one blow. Fly staggers out of the smithereens, flexing its wings in a daze.

"Stop it," Stanley Federglans whimpers, and looks around at an awed, silent bunch of spectators. The fly hops to The Astronaut's shoulder and rubs its eyes. "Thanks, buddy," it whispers.

"Now everyone follow me," says The Astronaut. He goes out the door. Each person is caught in his pose like a plastic soldier. At first no one moves but then, as when a traffic jam starts to clear up, and one car moves, and then another, and then two of them, and then five, until the traffic begins to flow again; or as when a tub of dishwater starts to lose its suds and first one bubble pops, then several more, and a crescendo of quiet popping bubbles, till the surface of the water is completely still, just a trace of scum; or as when during a riot a supermarket is looted, first the expensive meat disappears, then the overpriced canned goods and frozen foods, then the bulky packaged goods, until the store is empty; even so does the room begin to empty. They follow The Astronaut one at a time, and then several, and then a rush for the door as bells begin to ring for the down elevators. Stanley Federglans stays close to The Astronaut's shoulder, keeping tabs on what he now realizes is probably his former fly.

The entourage heads for Times Square. A new light fills the city streets, beige and pink. Everyone stops at the amazing space of Times Square, and all the faces gaze upwards in wonderment like the faces of a busload of tourists from South Dakota.

"Isn't this the most magnificent thing I have ever seen?" says the President's daughter, covering her blue-tinged breasts with her hands.

"What is this, somebody's publicity stunt?" asks a lovable derelict.

"Egypt on the streets of old New York."

"I can't believe it."

The Astronaut has led them to the base of the structure that now rests on Times Square, in the form of a pyramid that covers many square blocks of expensive real estate. Times Square has never been so silent. A granular dust that reminds one of sand blows against the base of the pyramid. People sift it through their fingers, remarking that it is almost weightless. No one touches the pyramid. It rises high above the skyline, out of sight.

"I told you I heard them building something," says a man from the vice squad to his cohort.

"It's all them Spanish-speaking people," the cohort replies.

The pyramid is steep, the faces smooth, of a uniform material with a dull luster, unlike polished stone or wood, unlike brick, unlike glass, unlike plastic—like dry ice, or more like fire, bleached and held immobile, consuming nothing.

"Well, do we stand here like lumps?" Mr. Benjamin asks The Astronaut, who has placed himself before the entryway. "Or do we get the grand tour? I haven't got all week."

"What's in there?" someone asks.

"Nothing, yet," says The Astronaut.

"I'll bet there's nothing. You've got Times Square in there."

The Astronaut says nothing, doesn't move.

"You've got The Great White Way in there. Let us see it."

"I want a slice of pizza," says a balding reporter. "And I'm going to get it." He steps around The Astronaut and peers into the entrance. "It's not too dark," he says to the others. He takes a tentative step inside the doorway. The rest begin to follow, crowding at the entrance. The Astronaut stands aside, and as dishwater disappears down a drain, or as cars after the last show pull out of a drive-in theater, leaving a slight smell of exhaust, even more swiftly does everyone disappear into the pyramid. Then the door over the entrance closes like an upper lip, and a slurping sound fills the interior, barely audible from the outside.

The fly leaves The Astronaut's shoulder and

lands on the doorway. "You are a perfect buddy," says the fly.

"It was a snap and an obligation," says The Astronaut. "So many fleeting dreams."

The Astronaut feels a light tap on his shoulder and turns to see a small policeman with his pen poised over a book of summonses. "You got a permit to park that thing on the city street?" asks the cop.

"I didn't think I needed a permit, officer."

"Everyone needs a permit," says the cop. "Now you'd better move that thing, buddy, or I'm gonna write you a ticket."

The Astronaut grabs a corner of the pyramid, pulls it toward himself, and folds it up to the size of a small notebook, which he stuffs in his shirt pocket.

"That's better," says the cop, pushing The Astronaut out of the way of a cab that rushes by, its driver furious. "Don't let me catch you putting that thing up again, unless you get a permit."

"Not a bad cop," thinks The Astronaut, and he heads for Grant's to get himself a corned beef sandwich and a birch beer. The air inside smells sweet and greasy. He meets a dwarf there sitting on a stool, sucking down raw oysters.

"I wasn't born this small," says the dwarf. "I shrink. As I get older I shrink, and now the older I get the quicker I shrink." He slurps down a few more raw oysters. "These here are supposed to help it. You should have some or else you might start shrinking yourself. You look a little smaller. Here." The dwarf puts an oyster in The Astronaut's mouth. A guard is watching them, slapping a nightstick in his palm. "Good, ain't they?" says the dwarf. The Astronaut nods. "You gotta eat them regular. They don't give it much publicity, but soon everyone is gonna shrink. It's the air in this city that shrinks you, the pollution. Everybody's got to breathe. So now it's your turn to buy me some more oysters." The Astronaut reaches awkwardly for his wallet and orders the dwarf another dozen. "Okay, let's cut it out," says the cop. The Astronaut pays and walks away. "That shrimp hustles oysters all day," the cop tells him. "Must be an addiction."

The Astronaut returns to Seventh Avenue and spots his friend, Eileen, standing in the ranks of the demonstrators. He crosses to the island. "I quit work," she says. "Better in here than out there." She points at the people swarming up and down the avenue. "I hate war, especially this one." She touches The Astronaut's hair. "I thought by now you'd be so fed up with Earth that you'd be rushing off to another planet. It must be terrifying."

"Not at all. It's very boring, and at the same time it's baffling."

"That's just the way I feel," she says. "But you can leave." She pulls a small notebook out of The Astronaut's shirt pocket.

"I'm sort of committed to stay in LEROY for the time being."

Eileen looks over the little notebook. Printed on the cover in caps is the word LEROY. The notebook is empty. Eileen points at the word. "What is this LEROY that you keep mentioning?"

"Just everything. It's nothing."

"What do you mean, 'just everything! It's nothing'? You cryptic so-and-so."

"I mean it's LEROY. You're in LEROY. LEROY's in you. Just look anywhere and name everything you see—that's LEROY."

Eileen looks at the corner of Seventh Avenue and 44th Street. Nouns rush in to fill her skull—shoes, cops, people, smirks, lights, cracks, shadows, ties, glass, friends, noses, walls, buckles, halves, signs, knives, hair, kisses, stores, noses. . . . "There's too much. I can't do it."

"That's LEROY. Whatever gets onto the page, or even implied, or even omitted by implication. That's why we call it LEROY. There's too much to name everything all the time."

"Is there more than one LEROY?"

"That question is more complicated. Let it suffice for now that if it's not LEROY you can't know it, you can't name it, because if you can name it, it's LEROY, even if you can't name it, in fact. So you can't ask such a question."

"It hurts the brain like Philosophy 1. I'll just trust you."

The Astronaut and Eileen demonstrate

through the night, and through the next three days and nights they help to tell the names of the men who have died in the war. Eileen finally turns to The Astronaut, her eyes red, her eyelids leaden. "I'm embarrassed to admit it, but all this solemnity wears me out. What should we do?"

"Perhaps you should go home to sleep," says The Astronaut.

"A super idea, and you should come with me and we can take a shower."

"I would love to come along, but there's always the question of LEROY. I have to keep it going."

"But if you come with me, won't it be LEROY wherever we are, just the same?"

"Ah hah," says The Astronaut, and they walk off together. From just out of nowhere a fly drops down, lands on Eileen's upraised hand, and without making a sound, winks at The Astronaut. This is the first record anywhere, in entomology, history, or literature, of a fly who can wink.

EXPLANATION B

Stanley Federglans, though his name won't rise again in LEROY, did have a right to know what The Astronaut was doing in his office. That presence should be explained everywhere. The Astronaut shows up in LEROY like a clap of thunder in January. What logic will explain it? The Western Man, set adrift on oceanic dreams, in his material prison swaddles the mind with chains of logic. Just beyond the conclusion something vast lowers into an immense silence and makes great men mute. Why don't they subsequently shut up? Paracelsus, great doctor, chases truth like a demon, inventing its language on the way. Galileo turns his miraculous glass to the sun. Most rational Isaac Newton knocks off the principles of mechanics and then gives the rest of his life to alchemy and light, evasive, fickle, contradictions that will scald the brain.

And now I have to explain how The Astronaut got into LEROY. I'm too confused to keep quiet. The original world of The Astronaut is as different from ours as ours is from a sycamore's dread of the police state. What a thought. Both our worlds are situated here on the planet Earth, though neither is aware of the other, and why should it be? The condition of The Astronaut's existence in his own world is the obverse of our condition. Imagine yourself on a high mesa, the cliffs of which are slick, unscalable. Very few even dare approach the edge to peer over. Below is a vast, unriffled blueness like the sea, perpetually calm. The cliffs of our mesa extend through the blue, though it isn't opaque, beyond the boundaries of the visible. The mesa seems to float. We are on it. Below what is visible, The Astronaut's world extends in its own infinite variety. How else to explain it? You have to have faith. What we can perceive is what they can't. Material to us has no substance to them. Our breathing in is their breathing out. Does this help? Every analogy is too simple—the crest and trough of the wave, or the opposite sides of the coin. Imagine a coin with no perimeter, extending infinitely in all directions, and that coin slowly flipping over and over—impossible. Or as if there were suddenly no image in any mirror, and at the same time our memory of what happens in a mirror were suddenly wiped away, then the image we can't see nor remember would be precisely The Astronaut's world. How else can I tell you about it? It's the world you would see if you could stare through a slab of granite. We inhabit each other. They move through us and we through them in perpetual opposition, though even "opposition" is a misleading term because there is no common perceiver to make such a definition. Their night is our day, but their night is our night, too. It makes no difference. Our winter finds them on water skis, or maybe not. All these simple-minded notions of what is. Endless worlds inhabit our planet, numberless as eyelashes. We come into being with infinite possibilities, and the barest minimum of equipment. I'm not concocting a fantasy for you. The Astronaut hails from our Earth, but we still have to ask how he got here.

He "came through." Sometimes we get inklings of the "other side," as certain mystics pass into the light, as the Star of Bethlehem appears. Ask yourself how you got here to now inhabit that body. Are you comfortable? Will you stay on? No? You're leaving? Where to next? All that can be said about The Astronaut is that he "came through," like someone in a tight situation, someone we depend on, pushing beyond his capacity, beyond anyone's knowledge. He "came through."

Mindless growth, immense waste, indifference are the conditions under which his fellow beings live there beyond, poisoning their own blessed planet, which is ours, the Earth, though we luckily aren't aware of it. He took it on himself to scour the universe, as they know it, for a fresh planet, and as he got further out into the most distant galaxies his people's astronomical instruments could discern, he was actually getting further in, by a process you can understand if you think of what has been said; until he arrived at what he took to be the inner surface of their universe, that seemed composed of purest light, but which was actually the outer margins of our own dear capacity to perceive the universe. At that point he suddenly "came through" to our world, inhabiting our mode of being for the first time, putting on what we call flesh, parking on this planet which he understands to be the one he thought he left, but in some spectacular rearrangement. That's how he got here, and I expect you to be skeptical, but I know that if you take the time to think on it you will recognize the truth.

11

THE ASTRONAUT STROLLS WITH EILEEN

One warm evening The Astronaut takes a walk with Eileen uptown from Battery Park. The lights of New Jersey reflect off the harbor swells to make iridescent paths in the smoky air, like the Northern Lights, like the slime trails of a slug. Foghorns wheeze. Nobody wants to breathe. The couple heads up Broadway, through the lighted, empty financial district.

"It's a long walk," she says.

"Just put one foot in front of the other," says The Astronaut. She touches his fingertips lightly with hers. "It's been such a strange day for me," she says. "You know, one of those days when you feel something weird. Something's going to happen."

"Why don't you report it to me?"

Eileen looks over at The Astronaut. Her hand feels warmed by his, but that word "report" is like a touch of ice. Despite the intimacy of his smile for her, he seems strange. She always wonders if he intends anything peculiar but is afraid to breach the delicately wired connections of their friendship with a question that could short it out. She proceeds on trust, on Midwestern optimism. She speaks. "Like coming down here to meet you," she says. "There was this little boy on the subway who kept firing a cap pistol into his mouth. His mother finally got exasperated and took the gun from him. Then the kid pulled out one of those pocket-knife key chains, you know, with the N.Y. Mets insignia on it, and he opened the blade, and swallowed it. His mother just became furious and screamed at the kid that his father was in Vietnam, and his father had bought him that knife, and if he didn't care any more than that about his possessions she didn't care about him either. She got off at 59th and left the kid on the subway in tears."

"What did you do?"

"I had to meet you."

A roly-poly man in a blue sweatsuit jogs past them, wheezing and coughing. He raises one arm in greeting and heads up Broadway past Wall Street. "Where are we going?" asks Eileen.

"To Henry the Barber," says The Astronaut. He pats her hand. "What else have you got?"

"Who is Henry the Barber?" she asks.

"You'll meet him. What about your next report?"

Eileen presses close to The Astronaut. Some cars head down Broadway for the ferry. She feels very alone with him now, peculiarly secure. "I think I told you about that funny old woman who walks around my neighborhood with rags tied to her feet, and she has that pouch around her neck, and an ancient rabbit coat she wears all the time, hot or cold. Well, this morning I turn the corner onto Broadway and she's beating this old wino fairy, who wears green tights and always panhandles on my street, over the head with her pouch. The wino screamed, 'O you hag cunt bitch, you female, now you've spoiled it, you slut, you hurt me.' He was helpless. The old hag's pouch broke, scattering a lot of rusty nuts and bolts over the pavement. That seemed to embarrass her. She didn't even stop to pick them up, just walked away, hiding her face in her hands. She paused by another drunk who was passed out on a doorstoop, took off her coat, and covered him with it. Underneath she was wearing a pale yellow cotton dress. She walked on again. She had the figure of a slim sixteen-year-old girl."

They reach a place where the man who jogged past them rests on the steps to an office building. With his head between his knees he cries, "O my God, my God," and throws up. Eileen and The Astronaut pause and when he realizes they are there he looks up. "Don't stop for me," he says. "Keep going. My office is just down the street." A thin stream of blood leaks from the man's graying hairline and runs down his neck. Eileen shoves her hand through the crook of The Astronaut's arm and presses against him as they walk on. A group of young men steps from the doorway of a building and follows them up Broadway. The Astronaut tells Eileen to pay no attention to them. He cherishes his awareness of the softness of her breast on his arm.

"On Broadway this morning near my house," she says, "I saw this cab slam into a brand new Sting Ray at the intersection near the Shopwell, and the driver of the Sting Ray threw open his door and came screaming out with a blackjack and started beating on the hood and windows of the cab. 'I'm no dumb Texan,' he kept on screaming in his Brooklyn accent. There was a tall redhead in the car with him who looked like a high fashion model. She coolly got out of the Sting Ray by its opposite door, got into the cab, which was empty, lucky for her, and told where she was going. The cab backed up and swung around the Sting Ray, catching the open door and ripping it off its hinges. The man threw his blackjack down in disgust, jumped back in his car, and wheeled it around to park it by a bus stop headed downtown. He hopped out and went into the Shopwell. I thought about telling you, so I followed him. He bought some farmer's cheese, several cans of soup, and a box of chocolate snaps. He told the Puerto Rican woman at the checkout counter that he was a rabbi and would soon be going to Israel, then he left the store and disappeared down the IRT."

The Astronaut suddenly whirls around. Five young men approach them slowly. "God, I'm scared," says Eileen. The Astronaut snaps a twig off a bush in the concrete tub on the sidewalk. "Here," he says. "Bite this stick." The young men form a semicircle around the couple. Two more rush up to join them. Foghorns from the river. A firetruck clangs. Cars heading for the ferry slow down to rubberneck. "Try not to be afraid," he admonishes her. "Humans can smell fear and it makes them tough."

One thick-shouldered youth steps forward. "This ain't no safe place, mister, to keep walking around with a beautiful chick like that." He passes his arm in an arc through the air. "Deserted streets, mister." He gets up close to Eileen, and looks over every inch of her. The Astronaut looks her over, too. He agrees with the young man. With her long yellow tresses, a soft summer sweater, her micro-miniskirt, her sandals strapped up the calf, she is a superbly pretty little Earth-chick.

Another kid steps forward with a wallet in his hand. "Here's your wallet back."

"It's not my wallet," says The Astronaut.

"Yes it is," says the boy. "A touch lighter, but you can have it if you want it."

"It's not ours." The streetlamps flicker on.

"Then let's see yours," says another.

"That's not necessary," The Astronaut replies.

"You sure keep your cool."

For reasons no one on Earth will ever explain, the word "cool" causes The Astronaut to explode into action. Feet, knees, fists, elbows, forehead like granite, his whole body becomes a whirling, indestructible weapons system. Within 129 seconds all seven young men are hobbling away from the scene, carrying their wounded.

"I didn't know you had that skill," says Eileen, hugging his arm with both hers as they start walking again. "You looked invincible."

"If I am, it's not my fault," says The Astronaut. "That was my first human fight."

"You probably could have killed them all."

"Isn't that ridiculous," he says.

They pause, and she turns to him, and they embrace. She has never been encompassed by such strength of arms before, and has never felt this particular thrill in each vertebra and rib. "I'm so afraid," she says, clutching the back of his head and sinking her face into his shoulder. "Don't be," he reassures her.

"I feel some immense catastrophe on its way to disintegrate us all. We are so close to the end of everything."

"Don't worry, Eileen," says The Astronaut. "I can handle it."

"Do you really think you can? I mean, do you know you can?"

"Maybe I can," he says. "I don't see why not." He looks at her hands in his. Hers are long and slender and graceful and reddened from handling ice cubes. His are soft and chubby. "There's a good chance I can handle that and lots more."

It's night. The Astronaut leads Eileen down a side street to a small shop with a barber pole out front. The shop is closed, but a lamp glows in the back room. The Astronaut knocks. The lamp goes out and a shadow rushes between the two barber chairs. A bearded face peers at them through the door glass, and then the door opens. "You can come in," Henry the Barber says to The Astronaut. "But no ladies in my shop. Wait out there or leave," he tells Eileen. She protests. "Lady, miss, I'm no beauty parlor, absolutely not, and I'm closed besides. I do this as a special favor to him."

Eileen is angry, but she accepts The Astronaut's apologies, and they agree to meet later near her apartment, uptown. "Women's Liberation," the barber complains as they go to the back room. "After The Revolution I'm going to lead the male chauvinist backlash." Parts of bombs are heaped on a large table in the back room like the fixings for a salad—pipe bombs, beer can grenades, delayed detonation attaché cases. The barber is preparing a powerful charge to conceal in a potted century plant. He opens closets for The Astronaut that hold crates of rifles, ammo, grenade launchers, antitank weapons.

"Why do you show this to me?"

"It takes me a second," says the barber. "I know who to trust. I have faith in people. As a boy I used to raise canaries. I'm a gentle man. I used to earn money after school pushing an old lady around in a wheelchair. I worked in a logging camp. A bull-cook. That's where I learned how to hate women. She'd say, 'Shut up and cut wood.' I was exhausted." He takes hold of The Astronaut's sleeve and tugs him through the back door into a little courtyard where a ripe stench fills the air. "I want you to see my real pride and joy. I don't show this to everyone."

He takes the cover off a makeshift bin, and lights a match. The Astronaut covers his nose when he gets a whiff of the contents. "My compost heap," says the barber. "I figure someone will have to plant something after The Revolution. This is unique in the whole city, the only one of its kind." They go back inside and The Revolutionary shows The Astronaut a timing device of his own invention. "This is the kind of stuff you can't leave to the kids. They blow themselves up. You read about it. They're spoiled and naïve. It has to be easy for them. This is finesse, these devices. Look at the long hair they wear. How many of them read my pamphlet, 'The Patience of a Revolutionary'? Two a day? Less. I'm a barber, not an intellectual. Believe me, these are not the times for escape into ideas and fun. There's no time for companionable argumentation. Revolution is the only good idea. That's clear. Afterwards they can trip on each other's braids. But what's your name? I never saw you before."

"I'm The Astronaut."

"Wouldn't you know it. These days even a revolutionary has to make a living. Lenin ate food. Mao ate less, but he ate." The barber tosses something to The Astronaut from off the table. "A stick of dynamite. Amuse yourself. Of course, when I first got to this city not a cent did I have. I scrounged a little work here, there. I got a job selling encyclopedias and people thought I knew everything. I bought shoes. I bought bargains. I bought stockings for girls. I bought girls. Do you have an inkling of the corruption in a dollar bill? Who knew where I was? I slept in hotels, or in flophouses, or in my apartment house. I was an honest landlord. I would visit my friends at four a.m. and strip off all my clothes and roll around on the floor with their pets. They thought I was a lost cause, and maybe they were right, but I could see the misery and degradation of their lives. I vowed deep in my heart to do something to help them. I always remember the words of my grandfather, the old Wobbly: 'When things get worst, hope for the best.' That's just what happened, because I met the proud Cindy-Lou Van Eyck. She was a woman who if I met her today I'd shout 'hurrah.' She knew how to cuddle up to a man and give him strength. She was the one who first told me that if I have the talent to cut hair I should open up my own shop and become independent, and then flirt with disaster if I need to. 'Poppycock,' I said at the time. 'Sheer revisionism.' But now look at me. I'm cutting hair and living the revolution. Why? Because when I look out there and see the lovely human beings, my brothers, with heavenly minds of cosmic glory world revelations reading some newspapers I get pissed off. Someone should blow up the *Daily News.* They are hungry, little ones. They breathe poison, drink pollution, gaze on filth, while the rich have shiny things, eat pork, and play charades. Those are the truths revealed to me on April 14, 1957, when I woke up at three p.m. after a long snooze."

Henry the Barber goes on working as he talks. He sets several bottles on his table and fits them with covers and wicks. He grabs a five-gallon can from the closet. "All I ask of this life," he says, waving an empty Molotov cocktail at The Astronaut, "is to be allowed to live it simply, with now and then a good piece of cake, or a bag of cashews, dry roasted. I don't like them greasy. We are peaceful people who enjoy a good fuck. What can I do? I didn't ever ask to be a revolutionary leader, but no one appreciates a good haircut these days. The moment chooses its man and gives him muscle. Except for The Revolution, I'm practically out of business." The barber uncaps the gasoline and starts to fill the Molotov cocktails. Then he pauses. "Look. Smoke your cigarette in the other room. This isn't apple juice."

"I don't smoke," says The Astronaut.

"That's good. The Revolution needs every breath you've got. Now go in the other room and I'll take you to see The Wounded Comrade."

"Who is The Wounded Comrade?"

The barber doesn't answer, but gets involved in pouring the gasoline. The Astronaut retreats to the shop where he sits down on one of the professional barber's chairs. Outside a few women hasten down the street with children in their arms, casting terrified glances over their shoulders. Everything is quiet otherwise. The Astronaut thinks of Henry the Barber. Three times that week he had heard that name from the mouths of lovely girls wearing the loose garments of The Revolution. One of them handed him a sealed envelope with the address of the shop on it and a message within in clear italic script on fine white paper fringed with blue: HENRY THE BARBER. O the names, the names of men. World rides the names of men to its finish as on a stable of rare thoroughbreds: Buckminster Fuller Ho Chi Minh Joe DiMaggio Kennedy Marcel Proust Ron Sukenick Plotinus Philip Glass Muhammad Ali Baxter Hathaway Cesar Chavez Bud Powell Spiro Agnew Ray Charles Kate Millett John Cage Wernher Von Braun Raymond Roussell Golda Meir Dick Gregory Rudy Wurlitzer John Coltrane Bella Abzug R. Krum Sylvia Plath Bob Greenblatt and many others. Who among us is not on that list? Or why can't you be on that list if you have a name like that? Who does everybody think he is to keep you off such a list? You're no fool, or perhaps you are a fool, but what difference does that make? This world has changed since the era of the bare minimum requirement. We rap in those names like nails, push the finished box off to the side and sit on it, watching the wealthy women shed their privileges in The Revolution. They leave their worldly goods upstairs and stumble down to the scullery, mumbling the name of Henry the Barber, while he slaves over the revolutionary means and sweats out a justification of the hideous results. The Astronaut falls asleep and starts to dream.

"How do you want it?" asks Henry the Barber in The Astronaut's dream.

"Long over the ears, medium on top, and a wave's length in front."

"Sideburns?"

"Short."

Henry the Barber drapes a towel over the dreaming Astronaut's chest. "Do you mind the electric clippers?"

"Go ahead." The electric clipper starts to hum in his dream and he feels the warm heel plate touch his skull, just behind the ear.

"I have to ask you something," says Henry the Barber, waking up The Astronaut. He has put on a long gray raincoat, some black leather gloves, a narrow-brimmed black rainhat. He carries a satchel full of fresh Molotov cocktails, which he puts down in order to pump The Astronaut's chair up to its full height. "I want to ask you if you have tickets to see The Wounded Comrade?"

"What tickets?" The Astronaut asks from his height.

"You are right. Right you are. You don't need tickets. The Wounded Comrade belongs to the people," says the barber as he lowers the chair.

The Astronaut follows The Revolutionary past his compost heap, through an alley, onto an unfamiliar street. A wave of smell dense as carbide hits him like fear, and it's followed by the monotone roar of everybody mumbling. People rush past them, tipping their hats to the revolutionary barber. The intersection is packed with angry people and helpless, nervous cops. Up and down the street people are pressed together and furious. "Shit . . . come on and move . . . let's get it over with . . . no more of this. . . ." There's no air to breathe. The avenue smells like melting tar. "It's Henry the Barber," people say, as he and The Astronaut move forward miraculously, a little vacuole opening in front of and closing behind the great revolutionary and his friend, allowing them to pass through the crush like a piece of indigestible matter.

"Is it always this bad?" asks The Astronaut.

"This is good. What a turnout. All our people. I knew we could count on them."

"No one can move."

The barber throws his head back and laughs as they press on into an area illuminated by klieg lights, people's faces lit like the surface of the moon. Helicopters lower into the light, the wind of their rotors scattering banners and placards full of liberation slogans.

"That's him. Right there. There he is," a voice screams over a loudspeaker.

"Duck," says the barber, and they both drop to all fours and move on. Legs part for them as reeds for a canoe. The revolutionary barber knows his way past the high boots of the police.

Once out of danger they pause to rest, and Henry the Barber pulls a sandwich from his satchel of Molotov cocktails. He smiles at The Astronaut. "Is this what you expected when you came to see Henry the Barber?" He unwraps the sandwich and offers The Astronaut half. "The Revolution . . . this? You see how little we know. What will it demand next? The true revolutionary can refuse none of the demands the revolution will make on him. Revolution is not a dream, my friend. It's not a fancy structure in your head. It will remake your life, and you surrender your flesh, a mere pittance, to its truth. Your survival is the revolution. You must give up those cigarettes you smoke, my friend. The Revolution is not a dinner party, or like writing a novel or a string quartet or doing embroidery; there's no time for such refinement. It cannot be so leisurely and gentle, so temperate, kind, courteous, restrained, and magnanimous. I tell you confidentially it can be a pain in the ass." The barber takes a big bite of his sandwich and continues. "Look at me. The picture I had of myself was of the righteous, powerful leader who busts into the office of the big cheese, disheveled, grinning, a bandolier of bullets slung over the shoulder, my automatic weapon raised in one hand above my head. I was going to be the one who says to the fallen motherfucker behind the big desk: 'Enough bullshit, baby. The power is now with the people.' That was the revolution of my dreams, but look at me now. Revolution has asked me to crawl through this mob on my hands and knees, and so I crawl."

"Am I going to meet The Wounded Comrade?"

"You should read my pamphlet entitled, 'The Patience of the Revolutionary.' " The barber finishes his sandwich and they crawl off again. When they get out of the brightest lights they stand up. The Astronaut looks back at the brightly lit crowd. Garbage flies down on them from the rooftops, and huge objects. The wounded are screaming. A helicopter explodes and falls on everyone through the lights in a wheel of flames. "O help them," says The Astronaut.

"This is Christine," says Henry the Barber as The Astronaut turns around to find himself facing the loveliest girl he has ever met. She kisses him. She is slim as a roll of dimes, soft as the old couch. Her long auburn hair, her golden eyes, her lips sweet and slick. She wears the loose garments of the revolution. "I hope she becomes your favorite," says the barber. "She'll take you to The Wounded Comrade. This is as far as I go." He strolls off in his own direction.

The lovely Christine doesn't say a word but leads The Astronaut onto darker streets. They enter the lobby of a huge old theater. As crowded as it is in the streets, the theater crowd is tenfold. They pile against each other, balance on one another's shoulders, on top of the seats, under the carpets, they hang from the balcony railings, from the box-seat buds, from the high curtains. The air is fetid, full of smoke. Noise rushes around the hall like the scream of engines. People have heaped themselves in the center of the orchestra in a huge pyramid, climbing one another and gasping. In all the galaxies of his acquaintance The Astronaut has seen nothing like this. On the fringes people look stranded, desultory, bored. They converse blandly. They have nothing in common. They play double solitaire, eat marmalade sandwiches. They yawn. In a frenzy one of them rips off a piece of upholstery and rushes at the huge video screen.

Christine leads The Astronaut to the seat reserved for Henry the Barber. "Get an erection," she whispers in his ear as he sits down. She fondles him. His cock awakens. "Ooooohh," she moans as she lifts her loose robes and easily slides his penis into the warm pocket of her vagina, making an efficient use of the space allotted them.

An image appears on the screen, and but for the rumble of breathing everyone is silent. A man stands erect on the screen, bandaged from head to toe. He tries to say something through the bandages. A hand gripping a scalpel reaches over to slit the bandage at the mouth. "Unwind me," says the man. The bandages begin to unwind, revealing a fair man with dark hair, wearing gray leotards. He is healthy and unblemished. "The Wounded Comrade," he announces, after the bandages are gone. A huge string orchestra breaks into lush theme music as the image dissolves into a helicopter view of a street of low buildings. The camera slowly lowers, showing the residents leaning out their windows, gazing at the street below which has been converted into an outdoor hospital. Nurses scurry around among beds that are full of bloody people. The theme music shifts to a sprightly woodwind march. "These are the people's heroes," a voice proposes as the camera closes on a doctor finishing an amputation. As soon as the doctor saws through the bone a nurse snatches the leg and, smiling, holds it up for the camera. "This is the right leg of Comrade Marshall," she says. "He is doing fine." Christine squirms on The Astronaut's lap and leans her head on his shoulder, covering his ear with her mouth.

"Look at this," he says.

"I've seen it so many times," she mumbles.

The camera zooms in on a severely burned woman. "Comrade Marsha Fowler was burned by a downed helicopter and her pelvis has been crushed. She has a forty-three percent chance of recovery." The camera moves from cot to cot, picking out victims of interest. One man sits up and motions for the camera to close in, which it does. "I want to say hello to my mother, my wife, Susan, and little Tommy, and to tell them all that both my legs are fractured at the thigh and that I have lost the thumb and index finger of my left hand. I want to tell them I am quite happy." He puckers up and leans forward as if to kiss the lens, but the camera swings away in a blur and comes to rest on another makeshift operating table. Some sweaty doctors tuck in the guts of a man severely wounded. "Will this man live?" a woman interviewer steps into view with a microphone. The Astronaut recognizes her as Christine, who is softly moving on his lap. "This is Comrade Joe Kelly," says a doctor. "His colon has been punctured and he might have suffered kidney damage. If he lives he will recover."

The Astronaut rises from his seat and gently sets Christine down. She is asleep. A great wave of revulsion fills his human being. He makes his way to the projection booth and overwhelms the men working there and smashes the tape deck and projector. He rushes for the stage. The huge crowd slowly stirs in its somnolence. "You glimmer-freaks. There is no revolution on the boob tube. Human beings, leave this theater. Go back to the flesh. You can't defeat the powers of annihilation with your collective yawn. Witlessness has compromised your vision. Value your lives. Go home." Silence in the theater, and then suddenly, as a cube of sugar starts to dissolve grain by grain, people begin to crumble off the pyramid of bodies in the orchestra. They stretch as they begin to leave, some of them conversing brightly. Something refreshing enters the huge room. The Astronaut descends and moves among the people as if in a trance, chanting instructions. "Feed the pets. Wash the walls. Build shelves. Plaster holes. Take no shit. Organize. Get the truth. Clean the streets. Dig yourself. Read the books. Poison rats. Brush your teeth. Watch the daughter grow. Expect the time to come." Still chanting he moves to the street where the crowd has begun to thin out. An acrid residue of tear gas lingers on the air. Blood stains the pavement. As if clear water is bubbling up in a murky spring, the crowd disperses. "Follow men with knowledge. Strengthen the heart with silence. Learn the enemy. Study power. Oppose oppressors. Keep your share. Sole your shoes. Tend the children. Learn compassion. Mend the clothes. Befriend your neighbors. Gather bricks."

The Astronaut rushes to the shop of Henry the Barber, just as the great revolutionary is leaving. He throws himself into a barber's chair and leans back, breathing long sighs. "All right. Mow it off and be quick about it. I'm sick of this hair. Get to it."

"I'm sorry," says Henry the Barber. "The shop is closed."

"That's all right. Cut it anyway. I'll pay double."

Henry the Barber disgruntledly does as he is told, tying a coarse paper towel around The Astronaut's neck and covering his lap with cloth.

Then he goes around the shop, turning off the lights.

"No you don't," The Astronaut warns him. "You'd just better leave those lights lit."

"He cut your hair," says Eileen when The Astronaut finally meets her again uptown. They stroll down Broadway toward her house. "I have something more to tell you now, about what happened to me when I was coming uptown. I stopped off by Murray's candy store near the neighborhood where I used to have my welfare clients because I suddenly had a craving for one of his coffee egg creams. I was just kicking these cardboard boxes that were piled up against the wall when suddenly this old man with a long, yellowing beard pops his head out of a little cavern in the boxes and says, 'Lady, please. It's very disturbing.' I apologized and stepped back, and the old man crawled out. He stood up and stretched. He was wearing that yellowed long underwear that old men like. 'What time must it be?' he yawned. I told him it was almost nine. 'Nine,' he said. 'For some people, night. For me, morning. Gosh. I sure slept good.' He pulled an old tweed suit from the boxes and slipped it on over his underwear. 'Listen lady, excuse me. I don't know your name, but do you want I should sketch you a portrait of yourself?' I thanked him and said 'No.' 'I'm not fooling. I drew Bernard Berenson's portrait once in a flash when he was young and he sure liked it. He knew what would last, that guy. He's a dead guy now, but they still got the portrait. They were just sitting at a table at a café in Florence and I walked up with my sketch pad. I was wearing a beret. He liked it. He paid me good. He knew what it was worth.' I told him I thought that was wonderful, but that I didn't want my portrait done. 'Nothing to it. We go across the street and you buy me some breakfast and I sketch you. It costs you a little piece of steak.' I refused again. 'Nobody ever invites me for a meal any more,' he kept talking. 'I see lots of people getting out of the subways and going over to their friends' houses for dinner. Those people can get their meals anywhere with their money, but nobody invites me any more. I'd really enjoy a home-cooked meal.' I sipped on my egg cream. I wanted to get away from the old guy, but you know my upbringing. I was afraid to be impolite. 'I still don't know your name, lady, but if you won't let me sketch you at least I wish you would stay here and guard my boxes for me while I go get something to eat. That's such a little thing to do for an old man. Then at least I can feel secure about my boxes while I go grab a bite.' I agreed to watch the boxes as long as he promised to come back soon. I bought another egg cream. A half hour crept by, forty-five minutes. I finally decided to leave. With the housing situation what it is, I mumbled, there was nothing wrong with living in cardboard, but forcing people to guard it for you overtime was another story. First I decided to satisfy my curiosity, to take a peek in that little cave out of which he had emerged. I didn't expect to see anything, since it was so dark, but much to my surprise it was well lit in there. He had everything: a double bed, a dresser, a big wardrobe, night tables, lamps, and an original Persian rug. Everything he needed was there. No wonder he was worried enough to ask me to guard it. I was so enchanted by how snugly he had fit everything in it that I didn't even sense the crowd that had gathered around me until they nearly had me pressed flat on my face. I stood up, and there was a mob, of mostly kids, but a lot of my welfare clients as well. They chattered in Spanish, and their babies were crying. Bad vibes were whirling around me, so I backed away as they closed in on the cardboard. Pieces of it went flying all over, and the neighborhood people started toting off everything the old man owned. A small washing machine went, bathroom fixtures, even his bathtub, his easel, several rolls of canvas, his paints, all his masterpieces. I watched it all carted down the street into the poor homes of the neighborhood. I felt miserable. For one thing, he had asked me to guard the stuff for him; and for another, these were all my old welfare clients and I knew how poor they were. I backed into Murray's store, where it was quiet, and put my glass on the counter. 'It's terrible, Murray, what happens around this neighborhood,' I said. Murray was stacking some Danish on a plastic tray. 'Polluted money,' he said. 'The neighborhood isn't like the old days, when a buck was worth a buck.' "

Eileen hugs The Astronaut's arm and grins at him. "Well, that's my report," she says. "And besides having your hair cut what did you do till you met me?" The Astronaut tells Eileen the lengthy story of his evening with Christine and Henry the Barber. She pulls her arm from underneath his and walks alone at his side, a few feet away. For a while she says nothing. The Astronaut puts his arm over her shoulder and pulls her to him. "Did it feel good when she sat on your cock in the theater?" Eileen asks.

"What a ridiculous question. Of course it felt good. It felt damned good."

Couples rush past them to catch the last screening of Carl Dreyer's *The Passion of Joan of Arc.* The Astronaut and Eileen pause under the marquee near a publicity photo of the unearthly Antonin Artaud.

"Would you like to come to my place and see my new wigs?" Eileen asks.

"Your new wigs?"

A man standing near the box office watches them closely. The Astronaut glares at him. He steps forward and brushes some soot off The Astronaut's jacket.

"Who are you?" asks The Astronaut.

"I'm just a writer," says the man. "I find everything you say very interesting."

"You'd better be quick and alert," says The Astronaut.

They start to walk again, with the writer following a third of a block behind them, notebook in hand.

"Did this Christine have long hair? Was she pretty? How good do I seem after you've been kissing her?"

"Eileen," says The Astronaut, "don't be silly. I just saved LEROY from what could have been the worst disaster in history. It might have affected the whole world. I just saved the whole world."

Just then they arrive at her apartment house and she pauses outside. "What for?" she asks.

"What for? How absurd. What else would have been the proper thing to do in that situation?" The Astronaut spots the writer watching them from the corner.

"You and propriety," says Eileen. Her face takes on a mysterious and imperturbable pout that The Astronaut adores, a smile reserved at the back of her eyes.

"Yes," he says. "And the proper thing to do now will be to go upstairs and fuck."

They enter her house and push the elevator button. They embrace, grinding against one another, their tongues touching lightly. He unzips her micro-miniskirt and she steps out of it. "Next week," she says, as they embrace again. "Next week there will be a whole new set of problems that you will have to solve." The Astronaut tosses the little skirt to the writer observing them from the door of the house. The man grabs it and runs. The elevator is stuck on floor nine.

EXPLANATION C

The Astronaut was always in LEROY. It can't be otherwise. The problem was to discover him. It starts raining. Someone whips out a kite. Lightning strikes. Electricity shoulders its way into the nature of life. Discovering The Astronaut in LEROY is like flying a kite and the string slips out of your hand. "So long, kite." You wave, as your children sit down at your feet and cry. You promise them their next kite. They want to smoke the marijuana. Then one evening, one of the rare, clear fall Sunday evenings, you feel lively. You grab your telescope and rush to the roof to get a close-up of the Pleiades. The lens cap is stuck on, and try as you will to remove it, it won't budge. So you take your equipment downstairs, throw it in the closet, and tell your family you're going out to the Japanese restaurant. All of you. Your kids get excited at the prospect of raw fish. After dinner you stroll with your wife and kids down Eighth Avenue. Hookers, weirdos, thugs, commuters, fairies, tourists, queens, johns, cops, rapists, professors, rednecks, panhandlers, longhairs, fatties, pimps, preachers, bigots, top personalities all contribute to the education of your children between 56th and 42nd Streets. "That's where the old Madison Square Garden used to be," you tell the kids. They pause to look at the new parking lot in its place. Suddenly you whirl around and see your wife stepping into a cab with a chunky man in his glistening purple shirt and flashy double-breasted nine-button suit. The cab takes her away and you never see her again. You're standing in front of what used to be Madison Square Garden, the father and sole support of two kids whose security has suddenly been shattered. You have to figure out how to make a living and raise two kids at the same time. They're too young for school yet, and you can't afford a sitter with your salary from the Post Office.

"Madison Square Garden used to be real," you tell your kids. "That was where Rocky Graziano fought Tony Zale, circus, rodeo, horse shows, Carl Braun and Sweetwater Clifton for the New York Knicks, tricky Dick McGuire."

Your kids forget their mother instantly. They want to smoke the marijuana. You decide that it's a hell of a world and want your kids raised so that they can enjoy it. That's when you decide to become a writer. You have several reasons for making that decision: (1) It's easy work; (2) you can do it at home while keeping an eye on the kids; (3) if you play your cards right you can make lots of money; (4) girls like it; (5) you've always had a way with the words; (6) it can be satisfying to communicate the stuff from your heart to the hearts of other humans; (7) you might get immortality from it. Your first book, *The Exagggerations of Peter Prince,* is an enormous success and lifts you out of the doldrums. You go to Turkey with your kids in a

Land Rover and you camp by the Black Sea where you write a book of stories called *Creamy & Delicious* which is received in New York City with all its enthusiasm for monkeyshines and shenanigans. Your children bring back Turkish habits. After a brief rest period something comes into your mind which you call LEROY. Then something else appears in your mind that calls itself The Astronaut. You don't know what to do. The small fortunes you have made are dwindling. The aging gypsy woman you saved from a beating in Macedonia, who came back with you to America to care for your children, is suddenly asking for wages. The children are bitchy, feeling the pinch of their decreasing allowances. All at once it comes to you. You will make a fortune. All you have to do is make The Astronaut into the star of LEROY. Fortunes have been made on lesser inspirations. The Astronaut begins to fill the pages of LEROY the way fog fills a valley. You write at a red heat, never sleeping, keeping to the typewriter. Your children scream about your health. The gypsy woman, Estelle, keeps you going with a tea she brews out of herbs she gathers in the park. With a final, bruising effort, you finish the book—*Leroy: Starring The Astronaut.* Then you pass out. Your publisher believes it will be an astounding success, and he gives you a big advance with which you buy an island in the Bay of Northumberland and learn to fly a plane. What a bestseller that book becomes. You circle our troubled city in a new twin-engine Aero-Commander you purchase with the royalties. You are flying with your editor, your two children, and the gypsy governess. Everyone asks to see the parking lot that once was Madison Square Garden. You spot a young man through your bombsight sitting on the curb, reading about The Astronaut at an interesting pace. On him you release a shower of soft monographs pressed off the frosty lips of all the women you have loved to date, November 18, 1970. His delight pleases the planeload.

"All this becomes possible," you tell your kids, "because your father discovers The Astronaut and puts him in LEROY."

"Huzzah," shouts the editor.

At your moment of landing the telephone rings. You recognize the voice of your wife. "Are they yours," she asks, "those books I have been reading over the years and now so dearly love?" You tell her that they probably are. On the next day she comes over to get your autograph. You think it strange that she looks no older than when she left you, and that her eyes are now hazel and have a different type of glance.

"You are my wife, aren't you?" you ask.

"Why? Were you expecting someone else?"

You totter on the brink of unexpected feelings.

"I want to ask you how The Astronaut got into LEROY." She smiles.

"I can answer that for you easily; but you will have to promise never to leave, even on your most ambitious whim, and promise to finish raising the kids, to type the manuscripts, to bake the bread, to suck the cock, to answer the mail, to get the job, to drive the car, to make the money, to make the man feel good; then I can promise you an explanation."

"It's a promise," she says.

You stuff a Parodi in your mouth and pace back and forth in the room giving an anguished exposition of your life since she left you. "You see, in an indirect way it's your fault that The Astronaut got into LEROY." You look up to catch her response to the accusation, and discover she is gone.

3

A HOME-COOKED MEAL FOR THE ASTRONAUT

The Astronaut holds his nose by the river and watches the puffed bodies of fish drift down. They gather in eddies near the slimy banks, their nacreous underbellies scintillating in the smoky light. Up and down the river freckle-faced boys with fishing poles are weeping. He remembers the human dream he had just the night before in which there appeared to him a speckled trout, three river crabs, a pickerel, a small-mouthed bass, a yellow perch, a sunfish, a catfish, a sucker, a carp, and sixteen eels. They were all whistling a stupid protest song in a shallow pond, and when he decided to take a swim they all turned to towels, wiping him dry faster than he could get wet. "Such a ridiculous universe," he muses. "Galaxies screw it up. Stars and stuff screw up the galaxies. Planets screw up the solar systems. And then people screw up the bodies they inhabit. And then there's the gypsies, the Rosicrucians, the billions of comets barreling around, the asteroids, the motorcycle gangs, meteorites, comets whizzing in long parabolas, clouds of ions, buses full of mind-blowing freaks, exploding stars, trucks out of control, the everyday vagrant person without a cent to his name. It's more than anyone can worry about." The Astronaut turns from the scene of desolation in the river to the desolate scene of the city itself. Garbage heaps. Garbagy air. Folks wander around in the garbage, kicking it up underfoot, sucking it into their lungs, kissing it into each other's mouth. The Garbage

Age, not the Space Age or the Computer Age. Garbage fills everything: the oceans, rivers, the air; garbage bunches up against the curbs and flows onto the sidewalk, garbage lies against the trunks of the last few trees, garbage gathers in doorways. People leave their buildings, arms full of garbage to drop on top of garbage pails that are already stuffed. Garbage trucks cruise by with filth leaking from their seams and haul the garbage to incinerators that burn continually, dumping the garbage smoke into the air. The threat of inundation by garbage sends men squirming off into outer space, wearing ridiculous costumes; sets men to explore deep oceans in claustrophobic bubbles; and when they fill those outposts with wastes who knows what new heights or depths they will muck up? Man has the genius for creating dumps. Only Blathinger's garbage theory of creation, The Astronaut reflects, holds the phenomenon in clear enough perspective so the prodigious quantities of garbage can be understood. His book, *Waste and Rebirth,* explains with sheaves of incontrovertible evidence, his vision of the constant universe with alternating metabolic and antimetabolic eras in which the life of one era sustains itself on the garbage of the last. From that book many of the present-day garbage-worship cults originate. Blathinger himself suggests that the worship of waste is inherent in everyone in the following familiar passage from the book mentioned above: ". . . so we note that a man in a defecatorium will find it almost impossible to desist from taking a last look at his production, which he will admit smells foul, but is also disconcertingly appetizing, and it is not merely, as strict Freudians might suggest, that he is recalling his childish pride in his creation and hopes for the love of his toilet trainer, but every man can also see through this opaque mass into his own heapie ('heapie' is the Blathingerian term for the level of the psyche he defines as being far below the subconscious, a mass of primordial waste from which all things originate, in which everything still participates, a protean dungheap, the eschatological number one—Ed.) into the Ur-heapie, the origin of all manifestations of creation and consciousness . . ." Life persists, according to Blathinger, in a metabolic era such as the present until wastes reach cataclysmic proportions and smother all life in their own garbage, at which point everything rests for uncounted centuries until the new, antimetabolic forms appear spontaneously, an era of hydrocarbon breathers, munchers of minerals and plastics, with open sores that work like muscles, who communicate by coughing. At first The Astronaut thought the theory was just another crackpot idea until he himself began to have experiences in his travels that corroborated Blathinger. Evidence mounted in every galaxy, and his last trip capped it off when he discovered, on his brief sojourn on an otherwise barren planet, a huge mountain of lambchops tall as the Himalayas, but discarded as if they were nothing but waste and not worth at least $1.96 a pound.

The Astronaut descends into the stench of the subway. The walls are smeared with messages in lipstick: IF YOU DON'T THINK I'M PRETTY DON'T SQUEEZE MY TIT, L. M.; THE DINOSAUR LOVES TONY P.; FREEDOM NOW REBIRTH LATER. Three men covered with the *New York Times* are sleeping at the base of the steps, their lips fluttering against the pavement. A young cop prances nervously around them, poking at the bodies with his nightstick. He lives on Long Island. He has soft blue eyes and pale skin but for his neck that is rosy with frustration. The Astronaut pauses to observe. "Do you see these kind of bums? They'll wake up and call me a pig." The cop shrugs. The Astronaut decides to know these men. "The one on the bottom is Uncle Louie," says The Astronaut. "That one with his head on the roll of paper against the wall is Mister Burnham Fulton Jones, and the third is Mr. Jones' faithful editor and disciple, Sidney."

The young law enforcer looks at The Astronaut and then the sleepers and scratches his head with the nightstick. "You don't know these creeps. They lie around like a bunch of bums and you look like a normal person."

"You're wrong. I know them. They're just the kind of men who sleep when they're tired."

Wrinkles sprout by the young policeman's eyes as he squints to pierce the obscurity of a strange mode of life. "You mean they got no home to go to? No beds of their own to grab a night's sleep? No wives to make them coffee? What kind of a way of life is that?"

"It's just another way," The Astronaut explains. "To these people it makes no difference if they have all the comforts in the world. If they want a sleep they take it, boom, wherever they are. They're a new kind of people. I was with Uncle Louie here once when he was swimming at Cape Cod and got tired. He fell asleep in the water and woke up nine hours later, seventeen miles out to sea. It took him eight hours to swim back and he was so tired when he got there that he fell asleep again, immediately, on the beach, and if I hadn't been luckily digging clams nearby he would have been wiped out to sea again by the tide."

"O brother," says the cop, slapping his nightstick in his palm. "Have you been handing me a load. I suggest you just move along and I'll find these freaks a comfortable cell."

A few people rush up the stairs from a train, ignoring the sleepers. "Your jails are already so crowded. Why should you arrest them? Any minute they'll wake up and leave. Will you arrest someone who's just sleeping? What for?"

"Don't give me 'what for,' " says the cop. "These creeps have got vagrancy, and you've got being a pain in the ass to a police officer, so move along and don't assemble here." The cop begins to circle the sleepers again, pushing at them with his foot. "I said for you to move along." The cop glares at The Astronaut, who doesn't seem ready to leave. "Okay, what's your line of work, mister?"

"I'm The Astronaut."

"O Christ," says the cop. "Another fruitcake. So I'm the mayor of New York City. You'd better hop into your capsule and move, Astronaut."

"Why don't you let me wake them up for you first?"

"Blast off, Astronaut, before I scrub your mission."

"Give me one chance. I need to speak with them anyway."

The officer prods a few more times without luck, and then takes off his cap and fans his face with it. "What the hell. Go ahead. What can I lose? They're not getting up for me. But I warn you not to try any of your far-out stuff when they're awake. I'm a black belt, and I'm not afraid to use it."

The Astronaut bends down and starts to speak to the man he has named Uncle Louie. "Wake up, Uncle Louie. It's The Astronaut. Time to get up now. You're not supposed to be sleeping here." Uncle Louie starts to suck like a baby and then opens his eyes. "We have to wake up Mr. Jones and Sidney, too." The man stirs himself, slowly rising to his full height.

"What a whopper," says the cop. "He's a real beanpole."

"Uncle Louie is over seven feet tall," says The Astronaut, "and he's still young. He keeps on growing, and soon he'll be the tallest man in the world."

"I bet he'll still sleep in the subways like a bum."

Uncle Louie bends over to look the cop in the eye. "I sleep in the subway when I get tired in the subway. I got tired in the subway."

"The subways are filthy garbage places," the cop says. "Only the bums, the creeps, and the hippies would sleep here. Even Communists wouldn't sleep here, who don't want to work for a living."

"I beg your pardon, sir, but I should like to differ with you on several of these matters." Mr. Burnham Fulton Jones has been awakened by the argument and is meticulously stripping off the newspaper that he used to cover himself. His garments are fabulous: a carefully tailored five-button double-breasted white corduroy jacket, carefully creased narrow-legged deep-olive bell-bottoms with aquamarine pinstripes. Around his neck, between the gamboge wings of his collar, a magenta ascot made exclusively for him by Tum-Suden designs, glows like a landing light. "It happens to be an aspect of our belief, and I'm sure had we the opportunity to speak with you it would become an aspect of yours, that it benefits one to sleep wherever the notion of sleep assails him, especially if he should find himself in a filthy place with garbage about him and vermin crawling out, because we know the filth of our origin, and from the filth you awaken reborn. You have contacted the source."

"The sauce is right. You get the sauce all over yourself, haw." The policeman laughs at his own pun out of the right side of his smirk. "Now I don't care what you guys believe, because this is a free country. I don't care where you guys came from, or what they do there when they sleep. Worship where you please, even if it's in the garbage. But don't sleep like a public nuisance. This is a free country so you guys are free to get on a train and get out of here, or go back to the street, but no more sleeping."

"You're such a fine-looking young policeman that I would hate to wake up Sidney in his wrath for you. He has been editing my life's work and is very tired. This opportunity has been his first to catch a bit of sleep. He'll be enraged."

"If you don't get him moving I'll have to advise you of your rights and then you'll get to sleep in a cell."

"You might as well get him up, Mr. Jones," says The Astronaut. "Eileen has invited all of you for dinner. Aren't you hungry?"

"Hunger is my specialty," says Burnham Fulton Jones. "Uncle Louie, we'll have to wake up Sidney, but stay out of his way."

The tall man begins to rustle the paper around Sidney with his size twenty-four feet.

"Sidney," he sings. "Good old Sidney, wake up. We're going to have some eats, and the cop tells us to move."

"Please don't be upset, Sidney," says Burnham Fulton Jones as the newspapers begin to tumble. "This gentleman in blue is displeased that we choose to sleep where we worship. He asks us to move, so I suppose we must."

Out of the mass of paper like a mushroom from the leaves rises a fierce bald man parting his thin lips to release a growl. He glares at the cop with his one good eye; the other is made of glass with a six-pointed star for its pupil. He lifts himself from the rubbish in a long, ratty, brown tweed coat full of holes. Roaches rush around on the coat like swarming bees. He wears sandals cut from tires and his shirt is rotting at the collar. He salutes Burnham Fulton Jones and smiles, still growling, his mouth full of tin. "Who are you?" he asks The Astronaut.

"I am The Astronaut," he replies.

"You are fortunate. And who are you?" he asks the cop.

"You'd better just move along. I'm an officer of the law."

"Then you are the swine who interrupted my sleep," says Sidney, his growl persisting. "You awakened me prematurely, and that isn't advisable. You have cause to regret it, and your family will rue this day." Sidney swiftly draws from under his coat an enormous broadsword engraved at the hilt with the name "Heiligenschmerz," and before anyone can prevent him he lifts the sword high above his head and brings it down with terrifying swiftness on the right shoulder of the cop, cleaving the bones and splitting the young law officer in twain diagonally through the heart. The three men then rush up the stairs and down the street to the East Side.

The Astronaut bends over to catch the last few words of the bifurcated cop. "I guess that's the last time I'll ever try to wake up such a bunch of bums," is all he can manage. The Astronaut presses shut his eyelids and leans the head back on the newspaper.

"Now I have to catch the uptown local," he whispers into a dead ear.

"You guys leave quite a mess," the man in the change booth says through his coin hole.

"In this day and age, such terrible things happen," says an old woman changing a dollar.

"Who cares," says the raven-haired beauty next in line, patting her curlers.

The train is packed with people on crutches and in wheelchairs, all headed for Times Square. Braces, and elbows, and knees, and prostheses jab The Astronaut from all sides. When the train pitches a little woman grabs the back of his arm with her teeth.

"Sorry, sir," she says, letting go. "Otherwise I'm helpless."

At 42nd Street the whole crowd tries to exit, to catch the shuttle, and The Astronaut slowly loses his grip on the center pole as the mob presses on him in a clatter of crutches.

"Mister," one voice rises in his ear. "Why don't you just get out of the car for a moment so people can get by?" The Astronaut swings around, hitting the lady with his arm. "You son of a bitch," she says, lifting her crutch in the air. "I'm a cripple, but I'll brain you with my crutch."

The Astronaut grabs the crutch from her hands, breaks it in two, and tosses it across the platform. "My crutch," she screams. "You have destroyed my crutch."

"That's all right, lady," says The Astronaut. "Now you can walk good as new. Try to walk."

"I'm a helpless cripple," she screams.

"Just try to walk."

The lady takes some faltering steps and discovers her legs are sound as a colonel's. "I can walk alone. I can walk." Her voice deepens to a low tremolo. "I can jump. I can run." She disappears up the ramp after her crippled friends, without thanking The Astronaut, not that he expects to be thanked. He would rather not have done that thing, because he prefers to go unnoticed. It was a mistake caused by the ugly human emotion of frustration. In the future he would have to control such lapses.

"You're just terrible, that was awful what you just did," says a neat little man by his side, holding a black attaché case under his arm. "The least you could have done," the man frowns, but symmetrical scars on either side of his mouth extend from the corners of his mouth to just below his ears, to give him the appearance of a permanent smile. "The very least would have been for you to throw the broken pieces into the appropriate receptacle. You people come here from out of town and make our city filthy."

Eileen nudges a spicy hors d'oeuvre between The Astronaut's lips as soon as he walks in the door. She has made lots of goodies: truffled pâté, beluga caviar, spicy raw kibby, all spread on flaky crackers. Though The Astronaut confuses her, she really likes him, and feels herself "getting serious" about him. He is what folks in her hometown might call a "weirdo," and that makes her even fonder.

"I'm glad to see you again. We haven't been together since I quit my last job," she says.

"You quit again?" The Astronaut mumbles with his mouth full.

"It's not possible to work anymore. Nobody's competent to work anymore. I take a job and in two weeks I know more about the business than anybody else. They want me to work late, to work Saturdays, because all the starlets they hire foul everything up. I go bananas just because I can be competent in some stupid job. I don't care if the kids of America never get their Thread of Light Junior Laser Kits. I quit the job."

The Astronaut nibbles a bare cracker. "Now you'll have to hunt up a new job," he says.

"It's too late. To hell with it. I'm a changed woman. I can't find another job."

"How are you a changed woman? You've just gotten ridiculous, Eileen, since I've known you."

"It's because I know you that I'm a changed woman, and can never work again."

"What could I possibly have to do with any change in your life?"

"You don't work."

"How can you say I don't work? What I do is invisible to you, whether you know it or not."

"I know you're The Astronaut, and whatever you do doesn't seem unpleasant or difficult for you. Just because I'm a woman doesn't mean I can't do the same thing."

"That's crazy. Because you think I don't work you're never going to work again? How are you going to live?"

Eileen hands The Astronaut a last hors d'oeuvre and then flops down on the fluffy white throw rug near her couch. "I don't need to talk about it. I just want to be with you. I want to leave with you when you leave this planet."

"That's really a stupid idea. It's impossible. Do I have to explain to you that I'm not even human?"

"If we really want to, we can make it possible."

The Astronaut lies down beside her. "You are going to have to change your mind about that."

Eileen rolls onto her belly and her light cotton minidress hikes up to her waist. Her buttocks surface like a sunny shoreline. "When you eat the meal that I've cooked for you tonight you'll change your mind. You'll insist that I should come along just to cook your meals."

"You have no understanding of what happens to me when I change place. Eating is something that is done on Earth, not where I come from, and it is unlikely that it will happen again anywhere I go. If you understood all this rightly you wouldn't want to leave."

"You left your own planet."

"You don't even know that I have a planet."

"Everybody has a planet, silly. Besides, I really like you." She kisses him on the ear. "I'm very romantic, you know, and I'm sick of living on this horrible planet. It doesn't do anything for me anymore. Everybody's so mean to everybody else, and they foul everything up. And everyone's afraid. Maybe it's no better on another planet, but at least it will be different. And we'll be together."

"Listen, you are a beautiful crazy Earth lady, but you might not be able to breathe where I go next."

"I'll take that chance, as long as we're together."

"Let's stop this craziness," The Astronaut says, and he touches her buttocks, and then leans over to kiss her posterior ruga from her thigh creases to her coccyx, which he nibbles. "You taste good."

"Then you'll certainly want to take me along to provide that special nourishment."

"It's delicious being an Earthman," says The Astronaut. Eileen rolls over to kiss his face. "This is the last hors d'oeuvre you get." She plugs his mouth with her tongue, and then she starts to undress him and stroke his sex organs. She has begun to like the buzzing sound he makes whenever his cock is erect. It's like a hive of bees, or a massage machine, and his cock has a quality of heat she has never felt in herself before, and a kind of peristaltic expansion and contraction. Her vagina runs like solder and she comes and comes. "There's no one else like you inside me, peculiar and warm and active. It's like I'm blushing all through me. It's like being fucked by God, I mean it. I hope I make you feel good."

"There's no way for me to translate what I feel for you. Feeling itself is new to me."

"What a nice thing to say," she says. "Now let's eat like crazy."

"Okay, but you'll have to promise to remember that you're from Earth, Eileen, and I'm The Astronaut."

"And so you'll never know what it means to be a woman." She gives his cock a last caress and then straightens up to shake the wrinkles from her dress.

She has set the table elegantly for the two of them on a lovely rose damask tablecloth, with the amber glassware she has taken from her mother's home and the stainless steel settings of Finnish design. The candlesticks are a delicate blue-green earth glaze pottery, as are the compotes and casseroles, and for the centerpiece she has set up a tiny bonsai black pine. A bottle of Château d'Yquem sauterne, vintage 1934, rests in the silver wine cooler by The Astronaut's place, and on the table a bottle of Saint-Christoly 1964 in a wicker basket. The Astronaut remarks on the thirty years' difference between the wines.

"I quite like the younger red," says Eileen, "though the old sauterne has an immense reputation. We'll have him with the asparagus, the soup and fish, but you can open the other and let it breathe until the veal."

Just think about life on Earth, The Astronaut thinks as he settles down and pops the corks. All the different kinds of wine, with certain nuances every year. And you have a palate to taste it, and nostrils to sniff it, such inventions to abstract taste from the tedious business of life maintenance. A guy can meditate on taste alone. What a blessing is the whole battery of human senses, with the mind's capacity to abstract sensation from function, to delight in it, so being can appreciate itself. That happens only on Earth. Eileen can remember The Astronaut's sexual specialties without the fuddlement of procreation. She can tantalize herself with it, ready herself to snatch up each instant. Yet she meets her first Astronaut and wants to leave the whole kaboodle behind. What a curiosity. The Astronaut wishes there were some way to communicate the pleasures he is learning in the uses of flesh, of seeing, hearing, touching, smelling, feeling in the heart, pleasures he has found nowhere else in the universe, and never hopes to find, even in those realms of fulgent ecstasy to which he has been promised entrance once his mission is complete.

Eileen carries in two plates of tender, ivory-hued asparagus, laced with a mild vinaigrette. "This is the groovy 'Bergstrasse Spargel,' " she says. "You can't get better asparagus than what they grow between Heidelberg and Darmstadt. Once a year the little grocery store down the street manages to get a few pounds of it. He's German. He sells it by the stalk to his best customers."

"It's miraculous," says The Astronaut, lifting a white stalk in his asparagus tongs.

"Why don't you pour the sauterne," Eileen suggests.

The taste of the fine vintage, with its sweet edge, follows the asparagus over his palate just as a pretty young girl follows onto the dance floor the handsome boy she has been hoping would ask her to dance all through the evening of her first night at a discotheque. She never thought he would ask her, and now suddenly he has. Will she dance like a nymph, or will she turn out to be a stumblebum? The question need never have been asked. The sauterne and asparagus are a wedding.

Softness and peace settle on them in the room and the dimpled angels of appetite enmesh them in webs of smiles. "I feel as if we're already going off somewhere together, this is so strange and nice here, and so quiet. I love to cook delicious meals for someone I care about. I hope we never have to leave each other."

The Astronaut can't stop smiling. He has found no way to control the mischievous little emotions you get on Earth, that send the body off into unpredictable gestures: smiles, eight blinks, brow wrinkles, sweeps of the arm, jerks of the leg. "You're being too good to me, Eileen."

"I want to keep on being good to you in your spaceship, wherever it goes."

"You are going to have to get over your primitive notions about space travel, and who can do it, and how it's done."

"The only notion I have about it is you." Eileen clears the asparagus plates and rushes back to the kitchen, leaving The Astronaut with pearly sensations of well-being. He hears her humming in the kitchen above the whirr of the blender, and then she reappears with a small tureen set in a bowl of crushed ice, which she places in front of The Astronaut, and hands him a silver ladle. "The iced avocado soup," she says, with obvious pride. "Joanne Glass gave me the recipe. She swears by it, and I only hope I have lived up to it."

The Astronaut ladles the soup into two shallow bowls and passes one to Eileen just as the doorbell rings. "Who else is coming?" he asks.

"No one. Don't be ridiculous. I wouldn't ask anyone else. We can pretend we're not here."

"Okay," says The Astronaut, and they both sip a little of the cold, creamy yellow-green soup. It feels like plush in the mouth and stings like a whisper. The knocking at the door persists, increasing in enthusiasm.

"I can't stand it. I'll have to go tell them what I think." Eileen folds her napkin next to her plate and goes to the door. The Astronaut stares at the droplets of water condensed on the shallow bowl. "They say they're friends of yours," Eileen says, coming back worried.

"Who are they?"

"They sure are funny looking. I've never seen them before. They told me you invited them."

The Astronaut gets up from his soup and goes to the door. At first glance he doesn't recognize the men, but then he does. "He's here. He said he'd be here," shouts one of them, whom The Astronaut remembers as Sidney. "Waddaya know and waddaya say and waddaya mean and how the hell are ya? We finally got here," says Uncle Louie, who stoops down to get in through the low doorway.

"Please accept our apologies for the tardiness. As you can well imagine from the nature of our parting earlier today, we had much to delay our arrival. We were exceedingly grateful for your invitation and after much cogitation decided that if we don't come after all it would be tantamount to a personal insult," says Mr.

Burnham Fulton Jones. He steps into the room, dressed to the hilt in a pale velvet cutaway morning coat, his legs cased in narrow pants of rich umber flannel that set off a glistening blue satin shirt with frilled front; on his feet, lightly buffed moccasins of soft gray ostrich, and he wears a curled auburn hairpiece with a few locks teasing his ears. Sidney has shaved what little hair was left on his temples, and sports a fake black moustache. He has exchanged his ratty coat for a long black cape, and has set a strange moiré pattern in his empty eye socket. Uncle Louie is wearing tights stuffed with newspaper under a red waiter's jacket he has found, and he looks like a figure to be burned in effigy.

"It's good good good to see you again." Burnham Fulton Jones takes a hand of The Astronaut in both his own. "I was sure you wouldn't be miffed if we took the liberty to bring along a few of our friends to share our good fortune, and to meet you, our new friend. We even thought to bring along enough food to provide for ourselves and make a party of it." Sidney shoves the door open and lets in the fetid, grimy rabble of the streets that nobody loves. They drag with them some garbage cans full of steamy, putrid stuff, and plastic bags full of sodden trash. These are the exiles in our midst, the tainted ones, the maggots, men and women smeared with filth, drink-stench, vomit and excrement, the glorious dregs, limbless mutes toted around in sacks of greasy burlap by men with swollen eyes and running sores who scream at us and drool on us and we refuse to notice them, some cripples on splintering crutches, or strapped to dollies, pushing themselves along with their digitless wrists. The feculent mob squeezes into the room, each with a bit of swill for the party. They snort at their friend, The Astronaut. Gray is their color, gray their race, and their future is gray as their hands. They bring to the throats of Eileen and The Astronaut the unquenchable odor of the streets thick as incense. These are people you pass on the way to the theater, or to the dinner party, their hands extended. They seem to have no eyes. They are sheer population in your dreams. Your children imitate them, knowing the truth. They once were the parents, the doctors, oceanographers, first lieutenants, actuaries, pilots, programmers, stenographers, stock-car racers, artists, conservationists, and now they are united in the mystery of filth, massive poverty; they have let go of everything down to the skin.

"What are these creatures doing here? Who are they?" Eileen whispers fearfully in The Astronaut's ear.

"These are the people of your city," says The Astronaut. "You see them every day. You work around them. You should remember."

"I don't know them. I don't want them in my house. They're the swill, the garbage of the Earth."

"Amen to that," says Burnham Fulton Jones, and most of the group grunts in response.

"Are you the leader of this group?" Eileen

asks the one man who looks respectable to her.

"Of course not. There's no leader. Here we are, your friends."

Eileen pushes her face into The Astronaut's shoulder. "Such a stench. How will we stand the smell? They'll ruin our dinner. Please have them go away."

Sidney swings open the wings of his cape to reveal his prodigious arsenal. "We'll just stay here and amuse ourselves. You've got such a nice place, nothing to be ashamed of. You don't have to entertain us. You're being the perfect hostess." Sidney bows.

Eileen starts to laugh and weep like a woman to whom something wonderful has just happened. The crowd is flaked out all over her apartment. Three women whose faces look like they've been mashed into the sidewalk lick off their fingers that they have dipped in the avocado soup. They empty bags of garbage on her table and feel around in it for tidbits to stuff in the mouths of their red-eyed kids. "A silent butler," one man with a huge wen on his neck exclaims, and he empties a plastic sack of gray-green slop on her stereo turntable, yanks the wires out, and spins the mess on his lap, slurping up fistfuls and licking his lips. An obese woman dressed in a rotting tent sits down on the furry throw rug by the couch and sorts through the garbage the others dump around her from the cans. "This is good stuff. This is bad stuff," she says, making two heaps. "Great stuff," says a dwarf who approaches her. He looks like a moving wart. He pulls open the fat woman's tent flap to expose her pulpy, greasy breasts, and pours the remains of the Château d'Yquem he has found in the wine cooler down her cleavage, and thrusts his face down between the breasts to lap up the flow. The fat woman unzips his fly, flips out his cock, and jerks him off between wads of white bread.

The Astronaut holds Eileen's head against his chest. "We were having such a good dinner," she whimpers. "Now everything has gone wrong."

"Good old Astronaut buddy," says the huge Uncle Louie. "Now everything is okay, normal. You know what I mean. I don't express myself well, but this is great."

Eileen suddenly leans back and starts to beat on The Astronaut's chest. "You come to the Earth and these are the only kind of friends you can show me. These are the people you want to associate with."

"They're just Earth people. Why should I care?"

"Oh shit, my God," Eileen pushes away from him and rushes into her kitchen. The Astronaut follows. "My poached sole," she cries. "My veau milanaise." Burnham Fulton Jones is in the kitchen, emptying the pan of fish into a large sack of food scraps. "This is going to be exquisite," he says. "Perfect food." He heads for the veal that lightly simmers on the stove.

"Hands off the veal," shouts Eileen, grabbing him by the belt.

"Don't worry," says Burnham Fulton Jones. "We'll all partake. We're your guests, but we'll help distribute the food."

Eileen catches the meat just before he drops it into his sack, and after a brief tug of war it rips. The well-dressed man shakes his head. "I've never seen a hostess behave like this. Your indiscretion shocks me, mam'selle, and in front of our friend, The Astronaut. What opinion can he possibly have of us?" He drops his scrap of meat into the bag and leaves the kitchen.

"Here, taste it." Eileen hands The Astronaut a portion torn off the scrap she has managed to save. "Taste it. It would have been quite good. My butcher manages to find young veal." She shoves a piece into her own mouth. The Astronaut looks at his piece and smiles. Eileen is about to cry again. "What are you laughing at? Is that what you call cosmic laughter? Don't you have any feelings?"

"When you get mad you get close to the truth," The Astronaut says. "But remember that this is here and now. You have to accommodate."

"You talk nonsense," Eileen sobs. "Leave my house. Get out. Just leave me alone."

"Are you sure? You'll be sorry tomorrow."

"Just get going."

The Astronaut shoves his way through the slobs to get to the door. A man sits on a stool near the entrance with a notebook on his knee, jotting down his *aperçus*. "You ought to use a camera," The Astronaut advises. "You can never catch the flavor of this scene using mere language." He drops down the steps two at a time and rushes into the street to stick out his tongue. A bright patter of rain falls on the tongue, rinsing it clean, tasting sweet.

EXPLANATION D

The only proper explanation of what has preceded, at this point, is to admit to you that I am The Astronaut. This book is an autobiography. I can't explain it otherwise. If someone asks the question "Who are you?" my only correct response can be: The Astronaut. If I were someone else I would tell you. To clear things up somewhat I'll put down a brief account of some of the material out of my personal life.

Once when I was working as a lookout in the Clearwater National Forest and was on my way to get water for the day at a spring a mile below the tower, my little black and tan dog (who liked to chase bears and coyotes) suddenly stopped and began to whine and yip. I took a few steps more and then noticed a big mule deer in the trail, a doe with twin fawns. She was ready to kill me if I took another step. I was scared shitless.

Once I lived in Southern Italy, in Lecce, a sweet provincial city in the heel of the boot. I was poor and spent a lot of time walking around the countryside since I couldn't afford a bike. One day I set out on a dirt road to visit what I had been told was a small collective farm established during the fascism. At a certain point I noticed that I was being followed by a boy in his early teens. He was barefoot, his clothes were ragged, and his hands, much too large for his body or his age, were already rough, permanently inlaid with grime from his work. I stopped and tried to talk with him, but he spoke only Leccese, an impossible dialect. We stood there among some blue stones and olive trees, smiling at each other. He suddenly bent down and touched my shoes, then he squatted there for a long time, staring at my shoes.

Once I worked for a farmer near Windham, New York. I was a High School Farm Cadet, out of New York City. One evening when I was squatting and talking with him during chores I lost my balance and slowly fell into the shit gutter. The farmer was impressed with the slow grace of my fall. He laughed as if he had never seen anything so funny. When I visited him three years later he recounted that incident for me in complete detail, laughing with tears in his eyes.

Once Jingle and I stopped at Crater Lake in Oregon and stared at the blue water from the lip of the crater. Jingle was tired and pregnant and didn't want to go down to the water, so I rushed down the trail myself, touched the water, and then ran back up. I saw the same people coming and going.

Once, when I was still in high school, I went to Birdland four nights in a row and stayed from 9 p.m. to 4 a.m., listening to Bud Powell. I sat right next to the piano in the section that had no minimum and listened and watched without moving. Bud Powell, I thought, was the greatest living man.

Once, when I was in Istanbul, I sat on the

roof of the Hotel Sultan Ahmet, looking off at the Bosporus and writing in my notebook. On that day the Turks were demonstrating against the Greeks in the Cyprus situation. A parade passed by, five stories below in the street. Floats full of mutilated bodies out of papier-mâché illustrated what the Greeks had done to the Turks, or what the Turks would do to the Greeks. I turned around when I heard someone singing behind me. There was a Turkish woman on the roof adjacent, looking at me, smiling, and singing. I was alone in Istanbul and very horny. She was wearing a grubby blue knit dress and was shapely. Her face had a scar down one cheek, but she was exotic and sexy. She kept urging me to cross over to her roof. There was an abyss about eight feet wide separating us. She must have been a belly dancer the way she kept wiggling those muscles and calling me over. I didn't go. Fantasies of being beaten, knifed, castrated by her Turkish boyfriends bolstered my cowardice, though I did speculate that dying in the attempt to fuck a Turkish woman would make enviable jacket copy. I was back on the roof three days later and that woman showed up again, this time dressed in a shorty nightgown. I figured to hell with it, it was worth it, and I played Douglas Fairbanks Katz and climbed a water tower on my roof from which I could hop to a narrow ledge and inch over to drop off on her roof. From that ledge I could see not only the Bosporus, but the

Sea of Marmara. I was halfway along the ledge when several Turkish men appeared on her roof and stood there with their big arms folded on their chests. One of the men stepped forward and pointed to his temple and then at the girl to indicate she must be crazy, or I must be crazy. No one cracked a smile. I was scared shitless.

Once I went to a circus in Eugene, Oregon, that advertised a trained hippopotamus. The acts were generally boring and amateurish. When the hippo finally came out, its trainer led it in a circle around the whole arena and then back out the door. "It's hard," said the ringmaster, "to train a hippo to do anything."

Once I went with Ellen d'Alelio in Florence to a tourist bar near Santa Croce. When we walked down to this little cellar where there was some music a girl jumped up and rushed at me, saying, "Weren't we in Stuttgart? Didn't we meet in Stuttgart?" "Could be," I replied. "There are nine of us and we keep in constant circulation."

This doesn't give the whole picture. There are many more incidents I could relate to fill the vacancies in this autobiography, but I'll stop here. I am The Astronaut. I believe that the things that happened in my life never happened to anyone else.

7

CYLINDER

Eileen snaps out of sleep and tosses back the covers. The sanguine neon hangs in the air outside. Something moves up her leg like a roach and she swats it. "Hello," it says. "I'm the cylinder." Smaller than a cigarette.

"You won't be here all night, will you?" she asks. "I need my sleep."

"Definitely not," says the cylinder. "Staying ain't my nature." The little cylinder drops off her bed, rolls across the floor, and out through a slot it neatly gouges in the wall.

"That was cute," says Eileen, and she falls back to sleep.

Eileen empties the packet of mushroom gravy mix into her saucepan and then unwraps the chicken wings she can afford to broil for her dinner. "Broiled chicken wings in packaged gravy," she says aloud. At least there's still enough privacy, she reflects, so that she isn't overheard saying banal things to herself when she cooks. This morning she was standing on the bus next to a woman in pink who yapped away to herself continually. "B–19, O–11, O–5, N–7, G–1," she said. Then she looked clear through Eileen and grinned. "Almost that time. I missed the 'G.' "

A slight commotion in the bedroom. Perhaps someone was there who might have heard her say, "Broiled chicken wings in packaged gravy." What would such a person think? With the gravy packet in her hand she walks to the bedroom, reading aloud, "Wheat starch, flour, beef fat, hydrolyzed vegetable protein, spices, artificial flavor, salt, mushrooms, caramel color, beef extract." The cylinder is there, rolling slow. It has come through the wall, widening the slot it left last time. The size of a roll of quarters.

"Cylinder again," it says.

Eileen meditates in her bedroom every morning. She sheds this consciousness and rises out of the world of illusion, to explore the true nature of reality. As big as a roll of towels busts through the wall and rushes by.

"Remember me? Cylinder," it says.

Seventeen minutes pass before Eileen stirs herself. She stares at the hole in the wall. "That must have been peculiar," she mutters. Her super curses the Virgin Mary in Spanish every time she asks him to do repairs.

A fresh coat of gold paint on the mailboxes covers Eileen's name. "Buttons by the kilo, here," says the card she takes from her box. "I'm bathed every day, and eat *köfte.* Wish you could experience this." The card isn't signed. On the other side is a faded picture of two men in striped robes walking by a wall. One is wearing a tarboosh, his robe striped red and yellow.

He stares patronizingly at his companion who, with his arms extended so the blue and white sleeves of his robe hang down, is deferentially offering an explanation of something. At their feet, extending out of the picture, lies a small hill of dead pooches. LE MUR are the words printed in the lower right-hand corner of the card as a title or a caption. The postage stamp has been stolen, or has fallen off. What's left of the cancellation is a dull green smudge. "Edizioni El Musafir: Napoli," is printed between the message and address space.

Eileen puts the card back in her box when she hears the crunch and squeal outside. She opens the door to the street. The cylinder has grown to the diameter of car tires. It slowly grinds past.

"Cylinder. Hold up a second," she says.

"Tempting, but impossible," says the cylinder.

"You crushed that fireplug, that boy's trike."

Eileen reaches down to see if she can stop the cylinder, but draws her hand back when a moribund sensation, a sudden pressure of needles rushes up her arm.

"Cylinder," she says. "What are you?"

"Later," says the cylinder as it bashes into a pet shop window, making no noise, crushing the baby cockers and chihuahuas.

". . . old Gray Street is lit again if Jess hasn't

shot out the bulbs, but Pa's hog squeals a lot for keeping in town but he says it's like music so what can you do. Freddy is a clown. But I bet your teeth would still be white and pearly except for New York City. Billy bought the Dugan's little burro so cute but your sister's feet are worse. . . ." Eileen reads the letters from home when she rides the subway. It makes her feel interplanetary and secure while on her way to the museum. She looks up. A filthy, gray-bearded man is staring at her. His face is smudged with grease. The right pants leg is rolled up above his knee. "All the other children are hiding, except the kid in the corner with the moustache." He smiles at her, teeth ripe like cheese. He is a maniac. He doesn't stare at her, but hits on her with his opaque, honey-brown eyes. Eileen looks away. He moves directly in front of her. "That's what you say to them when they ask: 'How much do you charge to cut a throat, America?' " He forms his mouth into a perfect circle (his lips quite pink inside the beard) and lifts his chin to expose his neck to her. The train pulls into 42nd Street. He gets out. When the train starts again Eileen notices who the "kid in the corner" is. An old man, in a beret, with a big bristly gray moustache sits staring at his knobby hands. He pushes his lower lip over his moustache so it almost reaches his nose. Eileen gets off and surfaces across the street from the museum. Only a few people move on the street. The rest look blankly at the traffic that has been flattened to the pavement by some great weight. Eileen sees a familiar form moving away.

"Cylinder," she shouts.

The traffic has begun to move over its flattened precedents. Everyone stares at Eileen and, overcome by shyness, she enters the museum and heads for an exhibit by Lee Friedlander, her favorite photographer.

"How'd you get here? What are you doing? Why do you keep going?" Eileen, almost exhausted, trots beside the cylinder.

"Cubes stay still," it responds.

"Can't you give some warning?"

"Warning," it exclaims, speeding up.

Eileen sprints out in front of it as it heads for a crowded street. She pushes baby carriages and people out of the path of geometry.

"She's gone off her koogle," says a lady, snatching up her little yellow dog and jumping aside.

It clears a swath the length of the city and beyond, everything leveled out with hardly a sigh. Eileen is exhausted. "I've got some friends here," she shouts after the cylinder, halfheartedly. "People I love." She dries her eyes with some lace from her mother's heirloom comforter.

Eileen falls asleep against the wall of a building. She dreams she is standing in a long line at her bank. The man in front of her is good-looking, but the one behind her is a creep. As the good-looking one leaves she smiles at him and steps up to the window. She hands over her passbook and feels the hand of the creep slip through her armpit and touch her breast. "Hey you down there." A voice suddenly wakes her up. A woman leans out of a fourth-story window, shouting to catch Eileen's attention below. She holds a bundle in her arms. "Catch this one," she hollers, and releases the bundle. Eileen staggers backwards, still half coping with the hand on her breast in the dream. The wrapped thing wafts down, like a seed, spinning, and Eileen positions herself under it. The thing thuds into her arms and starts to squirm. Eileen suddenly hears a familiar sound coming from behind, like a huge foot squeaking in the sand, and she jumps aside just as the cylinder breezes by again, neatly demolishing half the building from which her bundle was dropped. Eileen trembles so much she has to kneel and set her bundle down on the freshly flattened place in which she now finds herself. The bundle is moving. She parts the soft flaps and finds a child inside. Embroidered on the blue flannel gown that covers the child's body is a message: ЯUOIVAƧ TИAꟻИI WƎИ ƎHT. Eileen is too weary to decipher it. When she is calm she lifts the child again and walks to the nearest window still intact so she can see herself holding it. "Lo," she gasps, when she reads the message reflected in the window.

. . .

She thinks she might be crazy. She's making it up, the cylinder and the flattening out. This time it goes by without a sound but grazes her from behind. She doesn't even turn around.

"You don't exist," she says, almost casually, over her shoulder. "You're in my mind."

"That would be relaxing," says the cylinder, almost out of sight.

The reality of the child is undeniable, however. Rouged, blue-haired old ladies stop her on the street to admire its radiance, and they often leave money in the carriage. Eileen has stopped working for money. In an eighth-hand Persian lamb coat ripped at the seams, and an argyle stocking cap, torn canvas shoes, she looks like a mendicant, wheeling her battered carriage up the street. THE NEW INFANT SAVIOUR beams under tattered blankets. She doesn't beg. People stop and leave her gifts, feeling better for it themselves.

"Can't you see what's happening here?" she asks an elegantly dressed young man who pauses beside her for the red light. "There'll be nothing left." The young man squints at her. His otherwise youthful face suddenly fills with wrinkles. He's nearsighted. The light turns green. His face is buried in his sleeve as he fumbles with his emerald cufflinks. He drops them in the carriage. "I hate the f . . . f . . . fucking things, anyway." The light is red again. He takes off up the street.

Eileen grabs the arm of a man in a leather jacket and tugs him onto the flatness left by the last pass of the cylinder. He follows her docilely, a bewildered grin on his chubby face.

"Can you see what's happening?"

"You've got sweet eyes." He tries to kiss her. She pulls away.

"Don't you ever look at what's happened? Don't you see?"

"Of course, who could miss it? I ain't dumb, miss. I don't know what you want from me, but I ain't no dummy."

With a sweep of her arms Eileen indicates the swath left by the last pass of the cylinder. "What can we do about this?"

"Not me, lady, I drive hack at night now, just to make ends meet. During the day I'm on strike. Five weeks we've been on strike now. I don't got it so easy."

"What if everything goes? What if that cylinder flattens it all out? What'll we do?"

"Look. Don't worry," says the man. He pats the child, and then Eileen on the head. "They know what they're doing. I'm sure they know what they're doing. I mean they're doing it, ain't they?"

The man rushes off. Eileen doesn't blame him. She's been living in this city long enough to know what it's like to be approached on the street by some apparent madman spewing his apocalyptic theories. It can push you over the edge. ЯUOIVAƧ TИAᖷИI WƎИ ƎHT rolls over in the carriage. He's growing.

. . .

"The baby doesn't cry. It eats well. Sometimes it gets so happy I just fill up with joy. But I've got to do something for myself. Why should it be my responsibility? I was just there."

"I can understand how you feel," says Hollie, one of the few friends Eileen still sees.

"Autumn is my favorite season. I want to be able to go somewhere nice."

Timothy, Hollie's boyfriend, sits in a corner reading Big Ass Comics and making noises. He is waiting for the conversation to end so he can take Hollie to a movie.

"Maybe we'll all go somewhere," says Hollie. "The leaves must be really pretty now."

"If the cylinder has left anything out there by now. It's all flat."

"Yes. The cylinder. Yes."

"Please don't patronize me."

"I'm not patronizing you, but sometimes you're not the easiest person to understand." Hollie catches her boyfriend's eye for a moment and raises her eyebrows. He sighs.

"I'm sorry. O God. I'm really sorry." Eileen grabs the child and rushes into the street. She hears it coming. Pears and apples and oranges fill the A&P fruit bins. She stands directly in its path with the child in her arms. The immense juggernaut fills the space between the buildings it crumbles down. She waits. "Hi," it says, big slowness coming at her. She lies down in its path with ЯUOIVAƧ TИAꟻИI WƎИ ƎHT folded in her arms on her chest. She feels nothing as it passes over her. "Thanks for being nice," the cylinder says, moving on.

"Now that was all silliness," says Hollie, who followed Eileen into the street. She takes the baby. "Brush yourself off, Eileen."

"Silliness? Didn't you see the cylinder?"

"Of course I did. I'm not blind."

"Well?"

"Eileen, if I stopped to worry about every strange occurrence I witness in this city, where would I be?"

"Now that's the straw that breaks the camel's back." Eileen takes the child away from Hollie. They are the only verticals left in the compacted wake of the cylinder.

The precinct captain sidles over to the table where, at the desk sergeant's instructions, Eileen has placed ЯUOIVAƧ TИAƎИI WƎИ ƎHT. He wiggles his warty nose, "Tootsie-wootsie." The baby punches away at the blankets that bind him. The desk sergeant is busy booking a line of freaks they have pulled in from a demonstration.

"Kiefer," says the captain. "What's this baby, here?"

"Checked it out, cap'n. It's clean."

"Well, do a quick asshole check of those freaks to be sure they haven't shoved a bomb up." The captain, a veteran of the Pacific theater in World War II, still fears the kamikaze.

"Why are you just standing there?" he says to Eileen.

"I just brought in this child I found."

"That won't help you, miss. If gooks use little babies as booby traps I wouldn't put it past you. We don't take those chances in my precinct. Line up there with the rest of them."

Eileen hastily tries to explain how this child has literally fallen into her life, and how it was a mistake to associate her with the rest of these girls, and that she had come to the precinct of her own free will. Her outlandish story seems even more far-fetched in front of a police captain. She realizes there is no hope in this police station to straighten out her identity.

"Cylinders. Floating babies. I ain't got time, lady. I ain't a shrink." The captain rushes out of the station house and two massive matrons push her into a small room where the other girls are undressing. "Sssssowww . . . sssowww . . . sssoww," they hiss. Eileen undresses. The matrons come back in with surgeons' gloves on their hands.

"Any VD or special infections?" they ask. No one answers. "All right. If anyone has it, she's gonna share it, dearies."

"Up yours, sow," says a little blonde girl with a women's liberation emblem tattooed above her breasts. The matrons grab her, bend her over the table, and shove their fingers without vaseline into her holes. The girl moans and hisses, "Ssssoowwww."

All the girls are instructed to bend over the

table and spread for examination. The matrons go through their clothes and their holes and then leave them alone in the room. Each of the girls understands that her arrest is political, and tries to convince Eileen that hers is, too. "It's no mistake," says a tall dark girl. "Yes it is," says Eileen.

"Of course it's not. Dig yourself like I did. Shit, I was never political till I met my old man." This slim redheaded girl sits down on the bench next to Eileen. "And you're so far out. I mean, nobody's gonna believe that story about cylinders and babies floating down from crushed buildings, because they're pigs. They don't care about you. They want to hang another roll of fat over their belts. Dig it. Pigs is pigs. You stick them and bleed them. You're from the Midwest."

A big round girl with a flowered smock over her leotards stops in front of them. "Like I'm beginning to dig being busted. It's outasight. You get to rap to people. You make friends. You learn Spanish. That's the pleasures of the police state."

The redheaded girl looks around the room. "Each of these women is dedicated to the liberation of the oppressed and exploited people of the world." She puts a hand on Eileen's arm. "You should understand your own position."

"Police are exploited people, as well," Eileen perfunctorily opines.

"Of course they are," says the fat girl. "I'd

love to ball that detective. Wilson. The black one."

"You've just got the wrong analysis of the situation," says the redhead. "We intend to liberate the police. We've got to educate them first. The way I see it, each offed pig is like four weeks of intensive study for them. They've got to learn that they're being used by a few thousand giant hogs that run the world so all the wealth accumulates in hogs' pockets. They're being used as buffers. They're being made to kill people to protect property. They've got to understand that they're just bodies that the hogs use to put between themselves and the people to soak up death. And to deal out death, which is the hogs' means of production, slow or quick. They take your life on the assembly line, or they kill you in the vanguard. You've got to get yourself together. Join us. Learn to make a bomb." The redhead laughs. Several of the girls are on the floor in various yogasanas. A deep, undulating OM fills the room.

"I don't want to make a bomb," says Eileen.

"Neither do I," says the redhead. "But I don't want to let them suck the life from me, and then fill me with the ridiculous substance of their materialism, to be wound up, like my father, with vague insatiable needs. Walking dead."

"That's a heavy rap," says the fat girl, parodying the yoga with balletic poses.

"Your rhetoric makes it sound too simple," says Eileen.

"You call it rhetoric. You want people to believe cylinders and floating babies, and you call it rhetoric. They ain't gonna believe you. At least we listen. Giving to truth the label of rhetoric is the last rhetorical defense of a liberal in retreat. Take time to think about what I said. You'll understand that it's true."

Eileen is almost relieved to have the conversation terminated by the matrons who split the girls up and take them to their cells. They ignore her when she asks about ЯUOIVAƧ TИAꟻИI WƎИ ƎHT. Four other women share the tiny space with her. Two Puerto Rican women hold a third up to the window so she can shout, *"Mira, Antonio, Mira,"* to the street below. The fourth, a young white girl, wasted, junkie, moves toward Eileen, her body shaking, digesting itself.

"You got a pin?" she asks in a voice like the scraping of flesh off a pelt.

Eileen has none.

"How about a bobby pin?" Eileen pulls a bobby pin from her hair. The girl sits down on the toilet with it and starts to scrape it back and forth on the floor.

"Hey . . . you . . . cylinder lady." The fat girl calls her from the cell across the corridor. "Don't waste time. Rap with them. Make them think. Organize." Eileen can hear the girls she was arrested with rapping in each of the cells up and down the corridor. Eileen turns to the Puerto Rican women. They ignore her. Some matrons roll the dinner carts down the corridor. "Chicken wings again," someone shouts. The white woman sits on the john, scraping at a vein in her arm with the sharpened bobby pin.

"Stop that," Eileen says, grabbing the woman's wrist.

"Get off me."

"You'll kill yourself."

"That's my business. Fuck off."

Eileen takes the bobby pin out of the girl's hand. "Not with my bobby pin, it's not."

"You shit fucking weasel Indian giver."

They slip the food trays into the cell. Eileen sits down in a corner and looks over the food. A slippery broth smells like sweat socks. Two chicken wings in congealed gravy. White bread. "This is the Sunday dinner," someone says.

She sits beside her tray. She feels neutral and numb. Up and down the corridor girls are eating and rapping. She could disappear. A rumbling sound begins, soft, in the distance, as if in her heart. She looks around. No one else seems to hear it. It grows. Soon it is greater in her ears than the sounds in the prison. She stands up. Can she be the only one who knows what's coming?

"Cylinder," it says, missing her by several inches.

"God, you're so big now," Eileen says, jumping onto the new flatness and following the cylinder along. "You didn't have to do all that just to set me free."

"I can't set you free," says the cylinder.

"You get everything. The babies, the helpless, the aged, wicked, innocent. You get it all."

"I get nothing," says the cylinder. "What passes under me is canceled. Cancellation, my métier."

"You spared me."

"I can't spare you."

Eileen hears a cry on her right. ЯUOIVAƧ TИAꟻИI WƎИ ƎHT is tottering on half a table in the halved precinct jailhouse. Eileen snatches it up and races after the cylinder. It's too far away, but it's grown huge, like something that is happening. She holds the child against her breast and it smiles. The smile, like a sudden precious jolt of peacefulness, settles on her heart. The city is flattened all around her in great wide bands. No one seems alarmed. People by the dozens ice skate at the municipal rinks. From the sheared tower of a nearby church comes the clang of half a bell.

"If it wasn't that I live in the back of my own store I never could have opened this morning. Across the street the bakery people live uptown and so that neighborhood goes and no more bread. That's that."

The flatness has taken on a pearly opalescence. Only a few islands of buildings are left in the distance. Eileen buys some milk.

"Who knows from where we'll get the milk from now on?" says the shopkeeper. "But you know what I'll miss the most? I'll miss the eggs. He comes in twice a week with real country eggs, like in the old days. The yolks are bright orange."

Eileen hands a cup of milk to ЯUOIVAƧ TИAꟻИI WƎИ ƎHT. He drinks from it as she walks in the street. A few people wander around looking for lost numbers. As Eileen crosses the street the cylinder flattens the store behind her. She's lucky she got some milk.

"Not much left," she says to the cylinder.

"Clear sailing," says the rolling one.

People sit on their stoops with some dogs that whimper and lick their paws. A few fragments of streets are left in the almond-shaped island of buildings still erect. Eileen walks with the child. All stores are closed.

"You may as well live in Brooklyn," says an old lady sitting on a heap of newspapers. She has drawn some lips on her left cheek with Revlon Jubilee Red. "There's nothing to do in this city, the way things are going. It's January, isn't it? Or is it March? This morning it was like winter and now it's midsummer again. You never know what they're going to do. You catch colds." The woman pulls her brassiere off from under her sweater and hands it to ЯUOIVAƧ TИAꟻИI WƎИ ƎHT. "Here. Play a little. Poor thing, it's a sweet child. Why don't you raise it in the country where you can be comfortable? Look at it. The spitting image of its father. People will start to live under water soon. I saw it on television. That would be something for your little boy. Television's now a thing of the past."

A dog howls as if the moon is full. A steady line of rats rushes along the foot of buildings, in and out of basements. Eileen hates to look the length of the streets to the edge of oblivion, so close now its opalescent shimmer lights the streets. She still thinks there's an outside chance that what she sees happening is just the grand finale to her personal paranoia. Is she making it up? Everyone she meets, if not specifically acknowledging the cylinder, is at least dazed by some undefined force rolling the whole kaboodle under. What could it be, if not what she knows is happening? The nacreous horizons close in like millenniums of sleep.

"Boh . . . bah. . . ." says ЯUOIVAƧ TИAꟻИI WƎИ ƎHT. "Peep beep paw. . . ." It presses its lips against Eileen's neck and sucks. She takes him in to Number 43 and sits down on a bench to feed him.

"Stand up now, put your face to the wall, put the child down." A man has followed her into the hallway. Eileen does what she is told. Indifference is what she feels to the consequences. What could happen?

"Turn around now." She faces a smiling, elegantly dressed man in his thirties. He's wearing his formal best. He holds a small, pearl-handled pistol pointed at his own temple. "If you shout, I'll squeeze the trigger. Promise." Eileen promises. He puts the pistol in her hand and directs her to point it at him. She does. He takes off his gold watch, several valuable rings, a ruby-studded St. Christopher medal; he empties his deep pockets of infinite cash, laying it all at the feet of Eileen. An old couple comes into Number 43. Their small dog runs up to the child and growls.

"Here, Spot. Come here, Spotkins. We're sorry. We left something in the apartment." They grab the dog and rush upstairs.

Eileen continues to hold the gun on the man as he starts to undress. He is well proportioned, slim but muscular. "This isn't the way I usually go about it," he says. "Normally we would get acquainted, and then we'd go to a show, and have dinner. We'd find out about each other. You really get little pleasure from it if you rush right into bed." He is naked. He arranges a makeshift bed out of his clothes on the floor, and then takes the gun from Eileen and points it at his temple again. He asks her to lie down. She does. She wears nothing under her dress. "You could be a very elegant person yourself," he says, kneeling down to kiss her thighs, her belly, tickling her with his little moustache, grazing her clitoris with his swift tongue. She almost forgot about sex, and is delighted to be reminded of it. His erection is long, thick, and firm. She touches it. She's glad that it's rape. He puts it at her lips, and she opens and they ease it in and slide it slowly, nicely back and forth. He has put the gun down beside her cheek. He lifts his chest off her as if to relieve her of the weight and she looks down to see his cock moving into her. He has a straight razor in his hand, the blade pressed against the root of his thing. She moans, she can't speak. He cuts it off like a reed, and lifts himself off her as if in ecstasy. "I never did that before," he gasps, and gallops into the street. Her lips close around the amputated thing. She pulls it out. It's still erect. She puts it with the rest of his goods near the bench and rushes to the door to see what has become of him. The cylinder has passed again, leaving little but Number forty-three standing in place. She can't bare to look at all the distance that has now been opened. Back in Number forty-three ЯUOIVAƧ TИAꟻИI WƎИ ƎHT has learned to back off the bench and crawl around. He waves the fresh penis around in his hand like a wand, throws it down, picks it up, touches it with his lips and giggles.

"Penis," says Eileen didactically, pointing at the object in his hand. "Peeee . . . nisss."

"It's too easy for words," says Eileen. Once she starts moving she keeps going in a permanent glissade towards the horizon, and the horizon never changes. Nothing varies. Whatever direction her gliding takes she feels nothing different. She tries to stop. She tries to go. An opalescent glow stretches everywhere. ꓤUOIVAƧ TИAꟻИI WƎИ ƎHT is thriving. She's a good mother. The child burps, speeding them up.

"Hey. Pay attention to where you're going," says The Astronaut, gliding her way after they collide.

Eileen doesn't want to look at him. "You say anything you want to get your way with a woman, and then you disappear. And then you show up again. You're like every other man I've met in this city. I've got a child to take care of. Now we're here in this dumb blandness. Let me think."

"Why don't we split for San Francisco?"

"I've never been to San Francisco. I don't want to go there."

"Honolulu?"

"No thanks."

"Liverpool? Pasadena? Ibadan? Parma?"

"Anywhere. It's all the same. Let's just go." She holds the child out in front of herself. "But what about him?"

"ꓤUOIVAƧ TИAꟻИI WƎИ ƎHT is perfect," says The Astronaut.

Off they go. Number seventeen opens the notion of gates like tonnage of eyelids lifting over warm passages. Number five twinkles beyond the altitudes and long numb vistas.

"Where are they?" Eileen asks.

"Just think of it."

"I feel so vague," she says.

"Let's move."

It's a long trip to Number three, but it doesn't take any time. They run into some chattering on the way, and once they are there, stickiness pervades, a quality of continual waking up. Close by is an escape into seven, cozy as someone else's home inhabited by smiles, by attitudes of comfort.

"Let's go to fifty-three," says The Astronaut.

"I can never make it," says Eileen. "But I do wish I could see thirteen again."

"Do you dare?" The Astronaut takes ЯUOIVAƧ TИAꟻИI WƎИ ƎHT from Eileen's arms and starts to teach him to walk.

"I don't want to seem foolish," says Eileen, lowering her eyelids.

"Then we're off to number eleven."

They accelerate along the infinite pearliness. What is speed? Eileen wonders. Where is direction? Are they moving? At every speed but one, Number eleven is unattainable. They hope to make several passes. So tedious. Do they wander? Where is color? she wonders. It's like trying to find that point at which a certain wave has disappeared into the calm of the Mediterranean.

"Mediterranean," Eileen says.

"What was that?" The Astronaut looks around.

"I want to go home."

Eileen pauses. ЯUOIVAƧ TИAꟻИI WƎИ ƎHT circles her, waving his arms and saying his first words, "Om hum."

A teapot sings. Breeze comes up. Eileen sits down on a sudden stone bench.

"I'd sure like to see color again," she says.

"That means you're tired of traveling."

"Whatever it means."

ЯUOIVAƧ TИAꟻИI WƎИ ƎHT stumbles and giggles in front of Eileen, insisting on his first words.

"Then this is the place to start." The Astronaut takes her hand and she rises from the bench. He places his palm in the small of her back and she gasps as if she has been suddenly emptied. Though they move downwards in a slow spiral to the right she feels as if she is being buoyed up into a rush of fragrances. Earth and cinnamon and lilac and coconut, all the scents she once knew; and a rush of bells, and the whispers of friends, and the heartbeat of her horse. "Om mane padme hum," sings ЯUOIVAƧ TИAꟻИI WƎИ ƎHT.

As if her eyes have been closed all along. The books. The endless fields of sorghum. Her hometown. Pink, green, yellow houses. White houses. Friends ready to go anywhere, anytime. She smiles at everything she ever knew stretching like the world in every direction. Her dream of life in the city is there. She takes her diploma from its frame and rolls it up. "So this is where everything is," she says, and nuzzles her favorite sheepskin coat.

"Don't let yourself be fooled again," he says,

and sits down at the controls, placing the child on his lap.

"But I just assumed that LEROY was done with," she says.

"LEROY is done with," says The Astronaut. "This is real life." He glances at the gauges, throws the thing in gear, and they blast off.

THE FIRST CHAPTER

Hot September days in New York City are the worst days of my life. The air is heavy and poisonous. I don't sleep at night, tasting the air, knowing I'd rather not breathe. My best spirit conceals itself like a spore. I can do nothing but find some air-conditioned places to hang out. Go to the movies. Go to a library. Go to galleries, museums: an urgent itinerary of "breathing spaces."

Once in a museum I become weird and lecherous. I follow girls like a mongrel on the dole, hitting on them in front of the Barnet Newman or the Jasper Johns lithographs. They have a million ways of ignoring me. They're right. Sometimes someone delightful and open agrees to have a cup of coffee with me and we sit down in the cafeteria. I look her over. Terrific. Dark eyes, little boobs, nice ass in soft velvet pants. The words from my mouth are tainted as the air I breathe. I want to fuck. I'm only bored by the situation, by myself, by the museum, by the lively girl from out of town with oxygen in her blood. I want to fuck. We stare in opposite directions as if we'd never met. I get up and wander off to another air lock elsewhere, trying to purify my mind with thoughts about this book. It's too late. The rotten air has made me horny and impotent. What is this gloom that has come down on the world? What girl can I possibly meet? What state of mind, or perfect lovely feature, or splendid active organ can she possibly offer to compensate for my desolation on these hot September days? I could stay in Dwaarkill with Jingle and my kids. And few temptations flow down the Dwaarkill below the window of my studio. Now it's autumn. Loud gangs of starlings rush upstream and downstream through the falling leaves.

I turned the corner of 57th Street and Fifth Avenue after spending as much time as I could bear in some air-conditioned art galleries. Though the air around it is generally pleasant, art is the most boring merchandise. Galleries turn it into pretentious knick-knackery. They divest it of surprise by making it too visible, too valuable, and too discreet in their fluky market spaces. As soon as I can see it I don't care about it. I don't want to be near it. It dulls the senses. What I can't see and what will never be told fills the world I prefer to inhabit. I stopped in at Doubleday to take a look for *Creamy & Delicious*, a book of short pieces of mine that was brought out in the summer by Random House, and then ignored. It made a lousy product. There it was on the shelf, shining brighter than all the other books, brighter even than *City Life* by Donald Barthelme. The store was air-conditioned so I hung out there and watched the shelf to see if anyone would pick up my book. No one did. A graying woman with a pince-nez and a plastic Doubleday name-plaque pinned above the right breast kept an eye on my grimy, suspicious presence. What is it to me, that book on the shelf? I rip around in the tuned delirium of my head, writing the thing down, and somehow the thing hoists itself onto a Doubleday bookrack. That wouldn't happen to a swan. September and hot and it's there on the rack and doesn't have to go outside to breathe or sweat. Is your bindery uncomfortable? I'll bite the neck of the first person who opens that book. The lady approached me, squinting over her pince-nez, curling her lip, about to say something. Enough.

I headed downtown on Fifth Avenue. Two people shoved leaflets in my hands. The Communists at the very helm of our government, the danger of nuclear war, the good shish kebab at Topkapi Restaurant. An old dowager looks at me and rushes down the street. Istanbul is another smoky city of paranoia where the food is good. Between 56th and 55th Streets I met Joan Jonas and Nancy Smithson with some well-dressed artist I didn't know. They didn't have time to talk to me. I could hardly fetch up a friendly word, so heavily was I defending myself from anything "out there" in the air. "I heard about you and the mushrooms," said Joan Jonas, as the threesome walked away. At the Museum of Modern Art I flashed my pass and they let me in. It was air-conditioned. I glanced at a roomful of photographs and then headed for the cafeteria. I sipped coffee and eyeballed some girls who looked cool in neatly tailored suits. I didn't exist. I returned to the room of photographs where I noticed a young blonde girl standing next to an older man. They leaned toward each other as if they were together, but soon the man left for another room. I became interested in the photograph just adjacent to the one she was looking at. She was nibbling on a piece of gray-brown root. "Is that licorice?" I asked. "It's ginseng," she smiled at me. "It's very good for you." "It's supposed to make you virile and potent," I said. "I don't need ginseng for that," she said. "It keeps you youthful, though. I'll never get old," she giggled. She told me she didn't drink coffee and was just hanging around till it was time to meet her sister. We looked at some more pictures. Finally she said she would sit down with me while I had coffee, if she could have some juice. We sat in the museum garden with two glasses of tomato juice. Her sister, she told me, was a book designer who lived in Brooklyn. I told her some tales of book designers and *The Exagggerations of Peter Prince.* She explained to me how healthy she was. I told her several stories about human health. The air sat on my eyes. She asked me if I was just a philosopher, or if I practiced what I preached about health. She kept leaning toward me as if we had become very intimate. I wanted to handle her. She smiled like a cheerleader at a football game in the snow. Blond curls jiggled on her head and down her shoulders. She was charming, containing a nice worldly poise in her natural ingenuousness. I felt like a prune. Joni Skreczko, 94 Wooster Street, Shelton, Connecticut, 06484, was the name she wrote in the little looseleaf notebook I usually use for recording mushrooms, or for jotting down occurrences of the Number 43. I left the museum with her, noticing, on the way out, a girl in a purple velvet miniskirt, with long black hair, that I might otherwise have tailed around the museum forever. We walked toward Sixth Avenue. "I walk very fast," she said. I was sweating. Moondog was standing on the corner of Sixth Avenue. I asked her if she knew Moondog. She said, "Yes, but I have to walk very fast." I stopped to talk to Moondog and she said goodbye and kissed me on the cheek. It was almost five, and the traffic was very loud. I had nothing to say to Moondog. I shuffled back to the museum to breathe in the lobby for some minutes. Carter Ratcliffe waved from behind the information desk. I took the F train to West 4th Street and headed for the Eighth Street Bookstore to cool off while watching my book on the shelf. Nancy Graves was there, looking over some books about the Middle East on sale. Nancy usually doesn't waste any time, but she was hanging out in the bookstore for the air conditioning. She told me about her new work. I often think about Nancy Graves in her studio, building life-sized camels out of wood, plastic foam, and goatskin, or making ancient skeletons, or heaps of bones, forelegs, hindlegs. The camels are great, mysterious art, and Nancy is an expert. She told me she was getting away from camels in her work. I left the store and headed for Waverly Place. No air. I turned and headed back for the Eighth Street Bookstore. The store was cold as ice water, cold enough to make me think about writing again. The book I was writing was tentatively titled *Leroy: Starring The Astronaut.* A cylinder suddenly rolled across my mind. I looked the other way and grinned in the middle of the bookstore. I wanted to rush back to Dwaarkill and write. Dave Burak, whom I hadn't seen for a year, came down the stairs with a copy of Timothy Leary's *The Politics of Ecstasy* in his hands. He looked spaced out, but tough, and even scholarly. I mentioned *Creamy & Delicious* to him. He waved the book at me, "You've got to expand your point of view. You can't always read Lenin." He told me that he had been in Chicago, working on the McLucas trial, and that they had scored a little victory. "That was no victory," said the severe young girl taking cash, her black hair pulled back from her head, a graduate of Sarah Lawrence. "That trial should never have been held in Babylon in the first place." Dave explained that they had prevented the death penalty, and McLucas was going to live, and they considered that a small victory. The girl sneered. "That's Youth Against War and Fascism," Dave said.

We went to the health food store down the street, the old one, where the owner has a gouty foot and overcharges. "I've been dropping a lot of acid," Dave said. His eyes had that puzzled jitteriness, like a kerosene lamp in the wind, but he still looked on top of it, full of bullshit, humor, and tact. "I was a Weatherman for a while, but I can't stick with them. They're too naïve about violence. They all were rich kids. That's why I'll follow Huey Newton to Vietnam." The little store wasn't air conditioned.

I told him that it had been a long time since I'd done anything political, and sometimes I felt guilty about it. He said, "Your books. That's doing something. You write your books."

I returned to my apartment on Morton Street. It was hot up there, full of New York City air. I stripped off my sticky clothes, lay down on the bed, and almost fell asleep. I didn't dare sleep. I pretended not to breathe and lay very still. People outside shouted in Italian. I tried to jerk off. When the guy who lives in the apartment below came home he put on the Beatles' *Revolver* album very loud. I decided to call George Schneeman, great painter and old friend, whom I knew when we all lived in Italy, he and his family in Taranto, me and mine in Lecce. Emilio, their youngest son, whom they call "Meemee," answered the phone. George wasn't there. He got Katie for me. She told me that George had stayed uptown to go to a movie because there was a party uptown for Lewis MacAdams' birthday. She asked me if I wanted to be her date and take her to the party. Dick and Carol Gallup were going up too, but they were usually late. I told her I would enjoy it, though I knew that I always feel like a distant cousin in the family of New York Poets. I hung up and fell asleep. When I woke up it was time to meet Katie, but I wasn't sure I wanted to go to the party. There was a football game on TV that evening, and I was ready to dissolve into that. I flipped a coin: heads was the football game, tails was Katie and party. It came out heads. I dressed and walked across town to meet Katie, glancing in the window of the Eighth Street Bookstore, where no one was perusing my book. She had on only a towel when I got there. The kids were running around. Avigail and Tō were sitting on the couch, where they had been sitting the first time I met them. They were going to baby-sit. There was no air conditioning in the apartment. Katie called Carol Gallup to tell her we would meet them at the party. We took a bus to 53rd Street. Lewis and Phoebe MacAdams were subletting Gerard Malanga's apartment. The party was full of poets. M.B. was there. George told me there was a girl at the party who said she knew me. The room wasn't air conditioned. There was gin and scotch and wine. Someone passed around the reefer. T.B. was there. L.W. was there. A.W. was there. P.S. was there. P.P. was there. "I think I should introduce myself to you. I was a friend of Julia Perkins at Cornell." The girl who knew me spoke. After a moment I remembered Julia Perkins. She was in a writing class at Cornell. She had a melodious sexy voice and funny teeth. I ran into her again in Rome a couple of years back and we spent some time together. She was gentle and bright and afraid just then of sex. P.S. asked me what I was working on then. I told him I was writing a book tentatively titled *Leroy: Starring The Astronaut.* Indifference surrounded his face like a balloon. D. and C.G. finally got to the party. I drank some more scotch. R.W. was at the party. J.C., C.D., J.A., K.K., A.G., none of those older guys was there. I realized I don't like parties of poets. They are too tall. I have to talk to their chests. Sometimes if they sit down I can bend over and say a few words to their smiles. I was drinking scotch and smoking. L.F. was at the party. R.G. and wife were there. I prefer parties of novelists. They are my height. Poets were looking out the window at the brightly lit roof garden across the street. It was done up like a jungle and might have been plastic. I felt a tap on my shoulder, and turned around. It was someone I didn't recognize, but who seemed to know me. "Are you R.L.?" I asked. The party wasn't air conditioned. "Not me," he said. "I am The Astronaut." "Beautiful," I said. "Isn't it about time we got out of here and went to an air-conditioned bar?"

On the way out I wished L. MacA. a happy birthday, and reminded him that I was S.K. "O sure," he said. "You know you look just like L.F. Do you know his sons?" He told some stories about L.F.'s sons, and then we left. We pushed downtown to a comfortable bar. The Astronaut was remarkable, instructive, more than I could have imagined. He spun some unforgettable tales about his many experiences around my head. People were lost in the smoke at the bar. I told him what I had written so far and he said it corroborated his reports to the letter. I was gratified. He told me many amazing things, some of which I have related in my new book tentatively called *Leroy: Starring The Astronaut.* Long into the night we talked, till we both were exhausted. The bartender closed the bar behind us, and we stepped out just as it was totally flattened. It was a surprise. Everything was flat, just me and The Astronaut as verticals.

9 781573 660464